Vampire Hunt

Dan Jolley

illustrated by Gregory Titus

GRAPHIC UNIVERSE™ · MINNEAPOLIS · NEW YORK

Story by Dan Jolley

Pencils and inks by Gregory Titus

Coloring by Hi-Fi Design

Lettering by Marshall Dillon

Copyright © 2008 by Lerner Publishing Group, Inc.

Graphic Universe™ is a trademark and Twisted Journeys® is a registered trademark
of Lerner Publishing Group, Inc.

Graphic Universe™
A division of Lerner Publishing Group, Inc.
241 First Avenue North
Minneapolis, MN 55401 U.S.A.

Website address: www.lernerbooks.com

Library of Congress Cataloging-in-Publication Data

Jolley, Dan.
    Vampire hunt / by Dan Jolley ; illustrated by Gregory Titus.
        p.   cm.——(Twisted journeys)
    ISBN 978-0-8225-8877-1 (lib. bdg. : alk. paper)
    1. Graphic novels. 2. Plot-your-own stories. [1. Vampires——Fiction.
    2. Plot-your-own stories. 3. Graphic novels.] I. Titus, Gregory, ill. II. Title.
    PZ7.7.J65Vam 2008
    741.5'973—dc22   2007043732

Manufactured in the United States of America
1 2 3 4 5 6 – DP – 13 12 11 10 09 08

ARE YOU READY FOR YOUR

Twisted Journeys®?

YOU ARE THE HERO OF THE BOOK YOU'RE ABOUT TO READ. YOUR JOURNEYS WILL BE PACKED WITH ADVENTURES IN A VAMPIRE'S CASTLE. AND EVERY STORY STARS *YOU!*

EACH PAGE TELLS WHAT HAPPENS TO *YOU* AS YOU DEFEND YOUR CASTLE FROM A GROUP OF MEDDLING VAMPIRE HUNTERS. *YOUR* WORDS AND THOUGHTS ARE SHOWN IN THE *YELLOW BALLOONS.* AND *YOU* GET TO DECIDE WHAT HAPPENS NEXT. JUST FOLLOW THE NOTE AT THE BOTTOM OF EACH PAGE UNTIL YOU REACH A

Twisted Journeys® PAGE.

THEN MAKE THE CHOICE YOU LIKE BEST.

BUT BE CAREFUL... THE WRONG CHOICE COULD MAKE YOUR UNDEAD LIFE VERY SHORT!

You look down at the long letter you're writing. You chew on the end of your pencil as you think about how to word the next part.

Vampires can look like practically anything. People only hear about bats, but we can change into a lot more than that. Sometimes how we look even depends on the people looking at us. You'll understand all of this better when you're older.

You're writing to your little cousin Marcy, who lives thousands of miles away, across the ocean, in a city called Cleveland. She's always so full of questions! Next time she visits, you plan to show her your alchemy laboratory, down in the second sub-basement. She ought to get a big kick out of all the cauldrons and test tubes. You sign the letter with a big flourish and a smiley face.

That's when you hear the sound of a vehicle approaching outside.

IT'S STILL DAYTIME, BUT THANKS TO SHADOW CREST MOUNTAIN, YOU'RE ALREADY SAFE. YOU GLIDE OUT TO TAKE A LOOK.

THEY'RE NOT TOURISTS. THAT MUCH IS OBVIOUS. YOU CONCENTRATE ON THE VAN...

...AND SOON THE NAMES START COMING TO YOU. VAMPIRES *ALWAYS* KNOW PEOPLE'S NAMES.

DANFORTH LATOUR.

MARTHA LATOUR.

GRACIELA LATOUR.

JASON LATOUR.

PROFESSOR ECCLESTON GUMPERT.

HARDLY ANYONE EVER COMES TO VISIT YOU IN YOUR CASTLE, HIGH UP IN THE JAGGED MOUNTAINS.

MOST PEOPLE THINK IT'S ABANDONED, WHICH IS WHY YOU DON'T BOTHER LOCKING THE OUTER DOORS.

BUT IT WOULD BE NICE, JUST ONCE, TO GET VISITORS WHO *WEREN'T* INTERESTED IN STICKING YOU WITH SHARP STAKES.

GO ON TO THE NEXT PAGE.   **5**

You're silent as morning mist as you move down the stairs. Cautiously you poke your head out over the banister of the grand stairway leading up from the entrance hall, and you can't help laughing to yourself. These "vampire hunters" always look so much alike!

There's the older guy, who looks like a professor.

Then there's the typical Hollywood leading man.

After him comes the beautiful young woman. This one seems pretty tough, though—she's holding a wooden stake—and she might know how to use it.

Finally, the two teenagers. Neither of them really wants to be here. You can tell.

GO ON TO THE NEXT PAGE.

You want them gone, of course. But what
to do with them first?

WILL YOU...

. . . taunt them, in the shape of a wolf?
TURN TO PAGE 14.

. . . just observe them, as a vampire bat?
TURN TO PAGE 18.

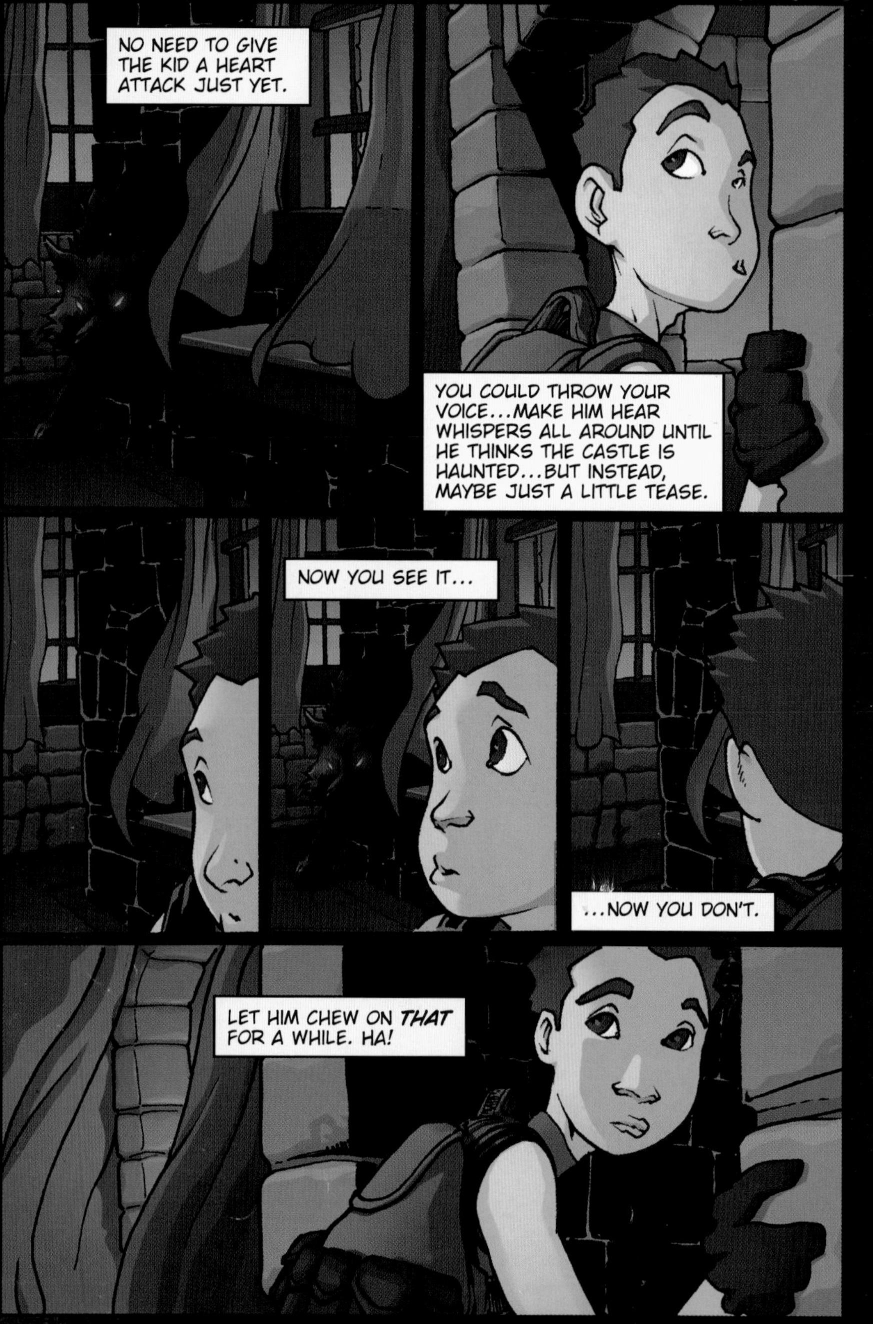
NO NEED TO GIVE THE KID A HEART ATTACK JUST YET.
YOU COULD THROW YOUR VOICE...MAKE HIM HEAR WHISPERS ALL AROUND UNTIL HE THINKS THE CASTLE IS HAUNTED...BUT INSTEAD, MAYBE JUST A LITTLE TEASE.
NOW YOU SEE IT...
...NOW YOU DON'T.
LET HIM CHEW ON *THAT* FOR A WHILE. HA!

GO ON TO THE NEXT PAGE.

The boy moves on unsteady legs back to the rest of the group. You keep watching him, out of sight in the shadows. *Poor kid*, you can't help but think. He probably thinks he's going crazy.

"You won't believe what I just saw!" the kid babbles to his people. He tells them about seeing you . . . or at least *thinking* he saw you.

The father comes over and tousles the kid's hair, then gives him a reassuring hug. "Don't worry," he tells the kid. "There may be wolves in the castle, it's true, but stick with us, and we'll make sure nothing happens to you."

GO ON TO THE NEXT PAGE.

"Promise?" the kid says. He's really scared.

The big guy nods. "I promise."

Martha moves over to Jason. She's about to say something, and you bet you know what it'll be. You've seen brothers and sisters before. She's about to tease him, or make fun of him, or do something to make him feel silly and embarrassed.

But then your wolf muzzle almost falls open in amazement. "It's okay," she tells him. "This is a scary place. I'm sure you did see a wolf, but even if it was just your imagination, there's no reason to be ashamed of it."

"Thanks, sis," the boy says. "I feel better now."

What? What's this? They're actually *nice people*? Why would a family of genuinely nice people break into your castle and try to kill you?

Vampire hunting is not a nice business, and if these people are genuinely good, you don't think they need to be doing it. But how to discourage them?

WILL YOU...

... scare them out of the castle so they don't waste any more time here?

TURN TO PAGE 67.

... talk to them, so you can explain how you feel?

TURN TO PAGE 70.

11

You let your mist-body rise up and grow more solid, until you've taken on a more human-looking form. Then you step out where they can see you. "Good evening, people."

All three of them jump. Immediately Danforth puts his two children behind him, staring at you warily. You raise your hands, palms out. "Relax. I'm not here to hurt you. In fact, I might be able to help."

"You just keep away from us, vampire!" the father says threateningly.

But the boy steps out from behind him. "What do you mean?" he asks. "How could you help?"

"Well, I know a thing or two about werewolves." The father and daughter flinch at the *W* word, but the boy's getting excited now.

"Your bite!" he all but shouts. "That's it, isn't it? The bite of a vampire can cure me of being a werewolf! I knew it!"

Your bite could cure him . . . if you consider becoming a vampire a cure. It's not a great choice for a young boy to make, but you do know you'd much rather have a vampire running around than a werewolf. *Nobody* likes a werewolf.

WILL YOU...

. . . offer to bite him?
TURN TO PAGE 75.

. . . offer to brew him up an anti-werewolf serum (that might have some unpleasant side effects)?
TURN TO PAGE 84.

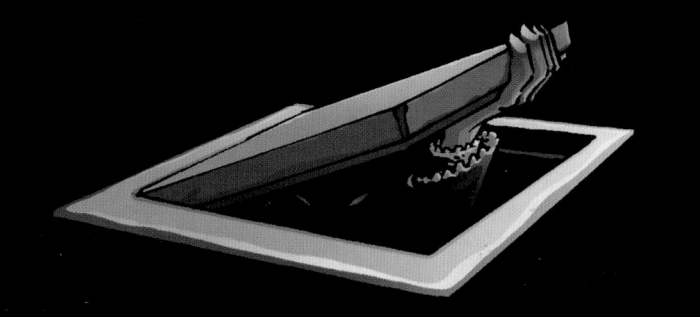

Your ears slide up toward the top of your head as your skull stretches out and your teeth grow long and sharp. Lustrous black fur erupts from your skin, you drop to four clawed paws, and a thick, bushy tail springs out from the base of your spine. You're now a wolf.

This ought to be fun.

The group of vampire hunters has moved into one of the parlors. You pad after them, keeping to the shadows. Your wolf ears pick up their conversation easily.

"Don't be silly," Graciela says. You think she's talking to one of the teenagers. "This could be the professor's greatest scientific discovery *ever*."

So they think finding a vampire would be a valuable scientific discovery? Hmmm . . .

GO ON TO THE NEXT PAGE.

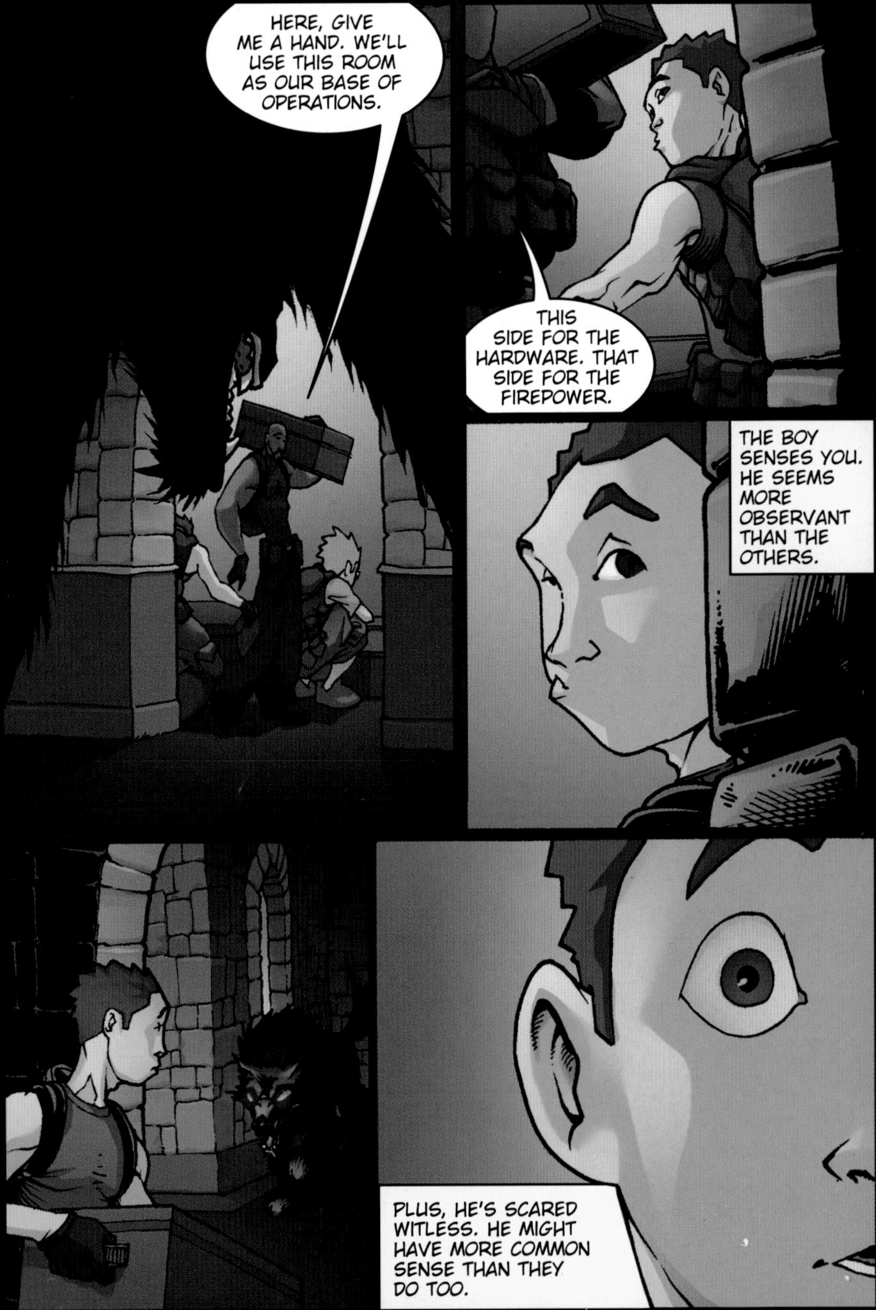
HERE, GIVE ME A HAND. WE'LL USE THIS ROOM AS OUR BASE OF OPERATIONS.
THIS SIDE FOR THE HARDWARE. THAT SIDE FOR THE FIREPOWER.
THE BOY SENSES YOU. HE SEEMS MORE OBSERVANT THAN THE OTHERS.
PLUS, HE'S SCARED WITLESS. HE MIGHT HAVE MORE COMMON SENSE THAN THEY DO TOO.

GO ON TO THE NEXT PAGE.

WILL YOU...

...give him the worst scare of his entire life?
TURN TO PAGE 58.

...keep things shadowy
and mysterious (and save
the real scares for later)?
TURN TO PAGE 8.

You wonder, as you run, where the family of vampire fans is now. You can hear their voices echo faintly from some distant part of the castle . . . and that gives you an idea!

Focaccia comes charging down the corridor seconds later. "I'll find you, monster! I'll find you and turn you into a *trophy!*"

"Well, then, look in here." Your voice sounds muffled, coming from the other side of a heavy wooden door. "I'm waiting for you."

"A-ha!" Focaccia snarls. "The vile creature has given up and means to surrender!" He jerks open the door and rushes inside . . .

. . . and then you push it closed behind him. Immediately he shouts from the other side. "What did you do? What is this?"

"I threw my voice," you tell him. "Now you're locked in my dungeon. Try to get comfortable, okay? You're going to be there a *long* time."

THE END

You know just what
this situation calls for.
Nimbly you leap up and
grab a heavy chandelier,
then swing your legs
up . . . and as your feet get
closer to the ornate metal
bars, they start to *change*. In
fact, your whole body started
changing the second you left the floor.
Getting smaller. Sleeker. *Hairier*.

Your ears grow pointed . . . and *huge*.

Your nose shrinks and draws back against your face.

Your fingers grow incredibly long and thin, and
leathery skin stretches between them.

And your feet, now small and clawed and strong,
clamp onto the chandelier.

You hang there for a few seconds, then let go and fly
silently into the shadows of the vaulted ceiling. Your bat
form is even quieter than when you turn into a wolf.

Now you can go and listen closely to these intruders
in your home. Find out why they're here and what
they want.

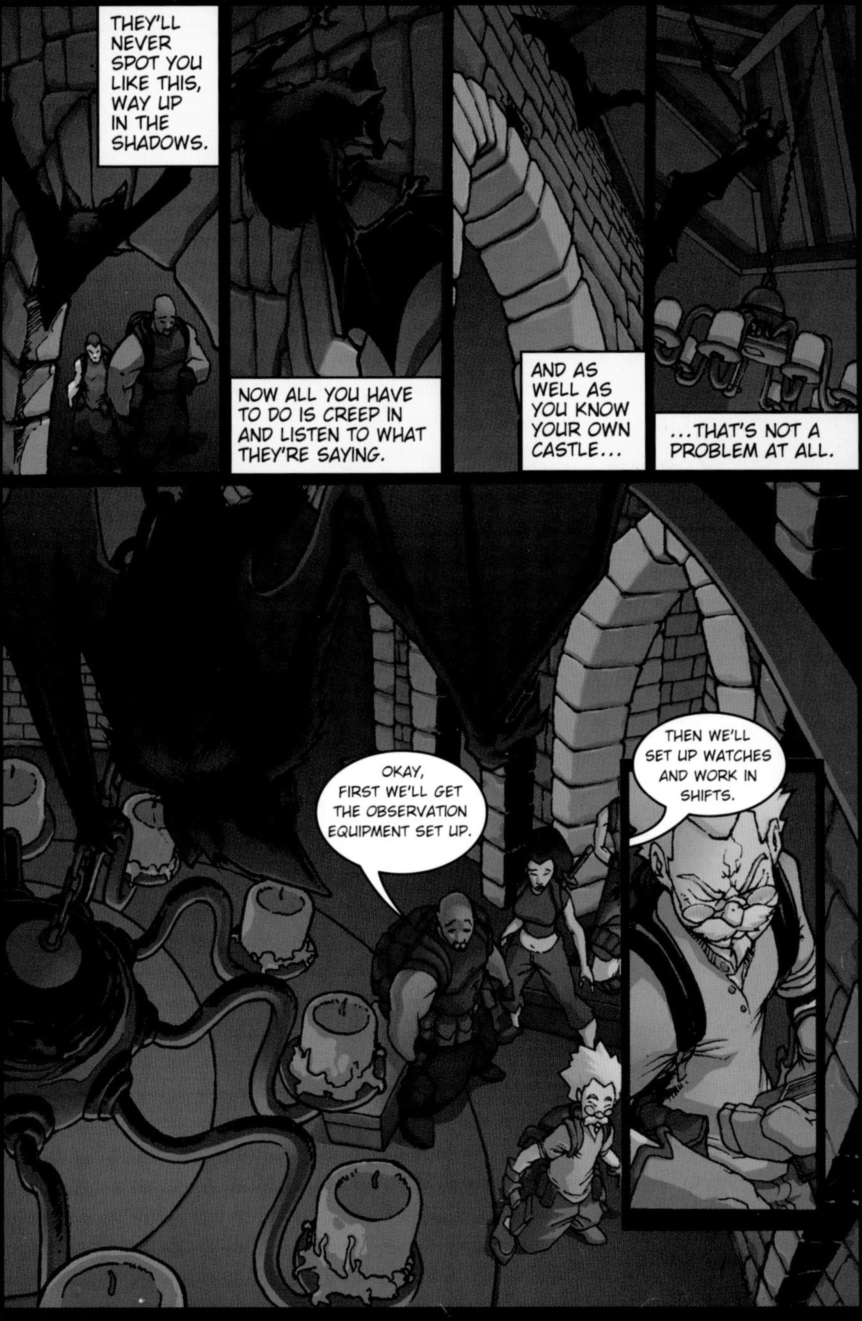
THEY'LL NEVER SPOT YOU LIKE THIS, WAY UP IN THE SHADOWS.
NOW ALL YOU HAVE TO DO IS CREEP IN AND LISTEN TO WHAT THEY'RE SAYING.
AND AS WELL AS YOU KNOW YOUR OWN CASTLE...
...THAT'S NOT A PROBLEM AT ALL.
OKAY, FIRST WE'LL GET THE OBSERVATION EQUIPMENT SET UP.
THEN WE'LL SET UP WATCHES AND WORK IN SHIFTS.

GO ON TO THE NEXT PAGE.

You could eavesdrop on Danforth LaTour and the rest of the humans with him . . . but the professor looks as if he might be up to something shady.

WILL YOU...

. . . concentrate on listening to Danforth?

TURN TO PAGE 27.

. . . follow Professor Gumpert?

TURN TO PAGE 72.

Slowly and carefully you rise up out of the van, your mistlike body solidifying. That was some crash! It's a good thing nothing in there could hurt vampires, because there was no way you could have protected yourself. Why, if the humans had had a rack full of pointy wooden stakes, chances are pretty good one of them would have ended up in your heart.

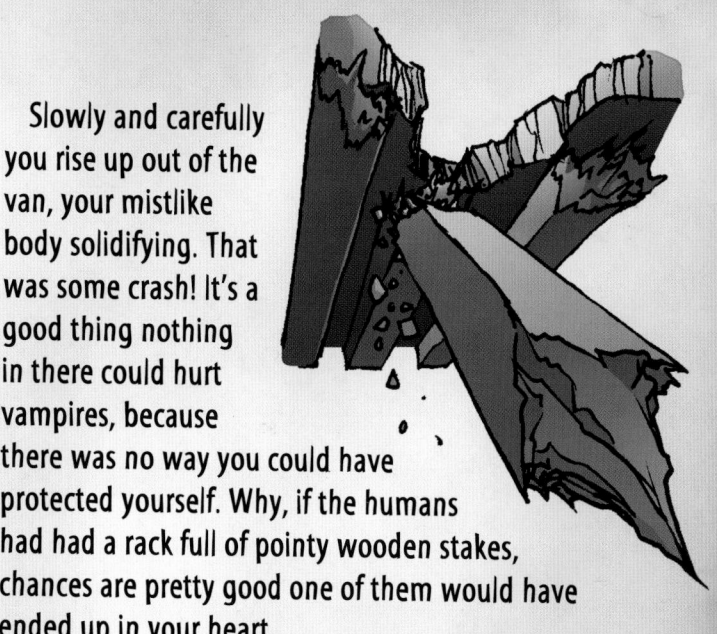

You come to rest on the top of the van and let your body solidify completely. After all, it's easier to be solid than vaporous. And that's when you hear it: a loud cracking sound.

It sounds like it's directly over your head. Just as you look up, a cracked wooden beam that the crash shook loose drops straight down toward you . . . and its broken end sure is long and pointy. Before you can move or react in any way, you realize that this is

THE END

YOU KNOW
YOU'VE GOT
TO GET OUT.

YOU'RE ENTERING A
VILLAGE, SO THERE
SHOULD BE A GOOD PLACE
TO JUMP FOR IT...

A-HA! COMING
RIGHT UP!

22

GO ON TO THE NEXT PAGE.

There—there's your chance! The van's about to pass right by a huge old church, and the building is blocking out the sun! If you can just make sure to dodge any crosses . . .

When the time is exactly right, you throw the back doors open and jump out of the van—

—and crash right into a wooden cart that you didn't notice before. The impact caves in the side of the cart, and the load the cart was carrying dumps all over you.

What is this? Why do you feel sweaty and feverish all of a sudden? You look down at yourself and realize . . .

. . . the cart was filled to the rim with cloves of *garlic*.

You can't move—it's too late. The garlic is all *over* you.

Your body starts to shrivel up, and there's no question that this is

THE END

You sit tight, waiting and watching. You know the sun is bright outside—you can feel the heat of it on the walls of the van.

You've seen a lot of things in your lifetime. After all, you're eight hundred years old. But you don't know if you've ever run into anybody as nasty and evil as this professor. The absolute first chance you get, you have to jump out of this van and get back to the castle.

After what feels like weeks (but is probably only about ten minutes), the van enters a tunnel. You're out the back door in a flash and then down a storm drain to the sewers. The sewers connect to an old network of tunnels that other vampires dug in the area for just such an occasion. Soon you're on your way back home.

GO ON TO THE NEXT PAGE.

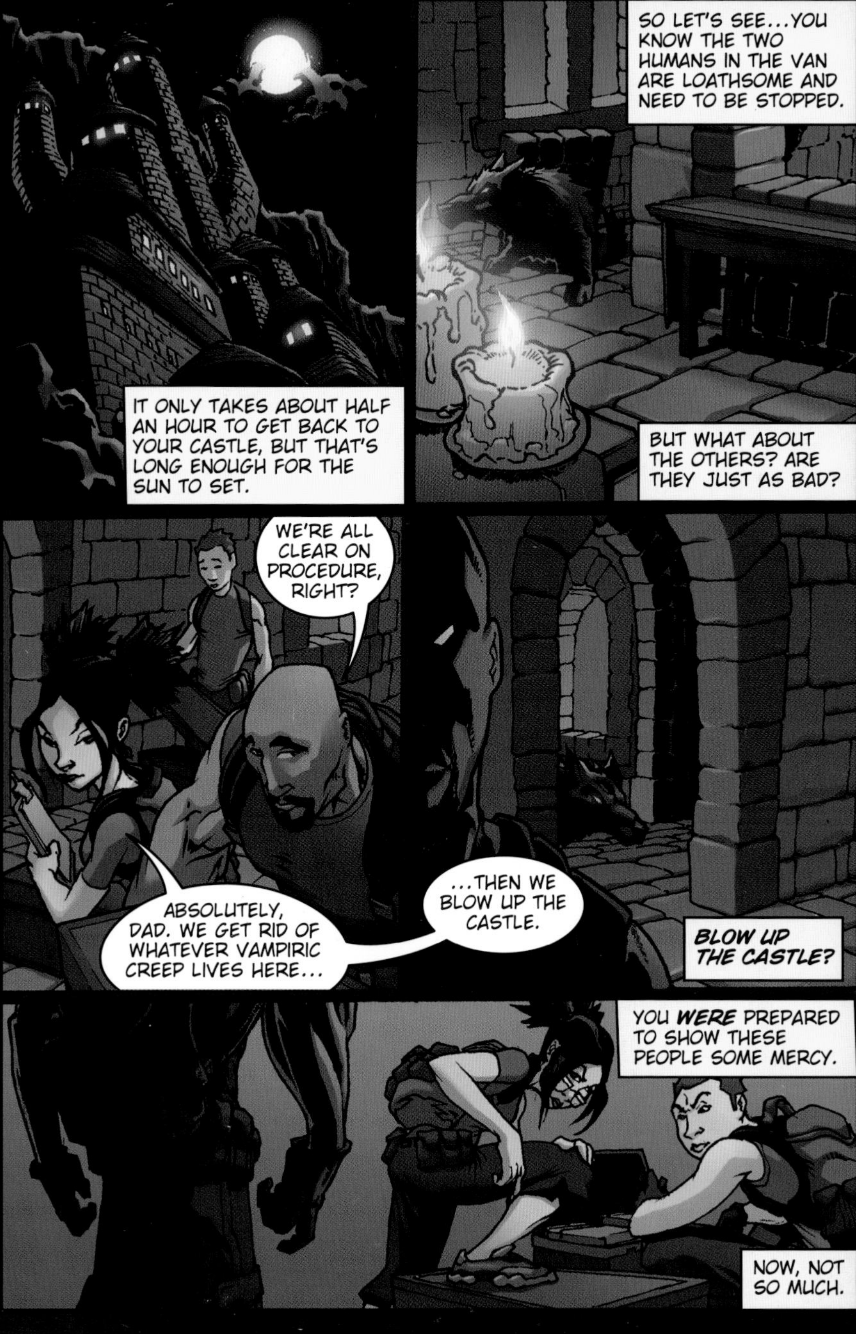
IT ONLY TAKES ABOUT HALF AN HOUR TO GET BACK TO YOUR CASTLE, BUT THAT'S LONG ENOUGH FOR THE SUN TO SET.
SO LET'S SEE...YOU KNOW THE TWO HUMANS IN THE VAN ARE LOATHSOME AND NEED TO BE STOPPED.
BUT WHAT ABOUT THE OTHERS? ARE THEY JUST AS BAD?
WE'RE ALL CLEAR ON PROCEDURE, RIGHT?
ABSOLUTELY, DAD. WE GET RID OF WHATEVER VAMPIRIC CREEP LIVES HERE...
...THEN WE BLOW UP THE CASTLE.
BLOW UP THE CASTLE?
YOU ***WERE*** PREPARED TO SHOW THESE PEOPLE SOME MERCY.
NOW, NOT SO MUCH.

TURN TO PAGE 45.

Where were they hiding all those guns, anyway? Oh well—it doesn't really matter. You've been behaving yourself up to now, more or less. But these people have come into your home—and now they're trying to *shoot* you?

You don't *think* so.

A terrifying growl boils up from your throat, and you plant your feet to prepare to spring. You figure you'll take out the biggest guy first and work your way down. You won't be able to dodge anymore, but who cares? Guns can't hurt vampires!

But then—too late—you realize these aren't just any ordinary bullets they're firing.

"How do you like my holy-water-filled ammunition, vampire?" The professor cackles. "Weren't expecting that, were you?"

As you slump to the floor, you can't help but admit it. No . . . no, you weren't expecting that at all.

THE END

IT MAKES SENSE TO LISTEN TO THE BIGGER GROUP, AT LEAST TO BEGIN WITH. YOU'LL LEARN MORE THAT WAY, YOU FIGURE.

ALL RIGHT, GRACIELA, MARTHA, YOU TWO ARE RESPONSIBLE FOR SETTING THE CHARGES.

GOT IT.

JASON, YOU DOUBLE-CHECK THE WIRING ONCE IT'S IN PLACE...

...AND BEFORE YOU KNOW IT, WE'LL BLOW THIS WHOLE CASTLE AND THE FILTHY VAMPIRE THAT LIVES HERE *SKY HIGH.*

GO ON TO THE NEXT PAGE.

They want to blow up the whole castle?
You've got to stop them!

WILL YOU...

. . . fly right down and attack
them immediately?

TURN TO PAGE 48.

. . . play it sneaky and try to
sabotage them?

TURN TO PAGE 35.

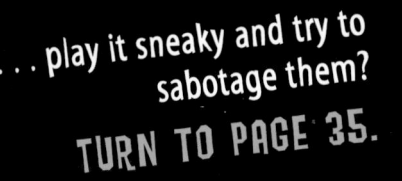

The police arrest Professor Gumpert that night. "But there's a vampire in that castle!" he tells the cops. "It has to be studied! This was the only way I could do it! You've got to believe me!"

As it turns out, the police *don't* have to believe him. The LaTours don't want to have anything to do with him, either, now that they know what he was planning for Jason. They all decide to head back to the States. Your work here is done!

Later on, you read in the paper that the professor was sentenced to a long stay in a mental hospital "for observation."

Couldn't happen to a nicer guy.

The Daily Times

PROFESSOR GOES BATTY, THREATENS TEEN

THE END

Silent as a ghost, you creep after the professor and the young woman as they climb into the van.

The mist of your body slithers through a crack below the van's back door, and then you're inside. The whole back of the van is filled top to bottom with super-high-tech sensors and communications equipment. Most of this stuff you don't even recognize.

Soon the van leaves the mountain's shadow, and you keep to the dim corners inside as red sunlight pours through the windows.

Then you hear the professor's voice from the front. "Your participation in my plan is most appreciated, Graciela." Hmmm . . . Becoming solid again, you grab one familiar thing, a microphone and voice recorder, and press RECORD. The professor goes on: "Even though I'm blackmailing you into letting me turn your son into a vampire, I really feel we're working as a team on this."

GO ON TO THE NEXT PAGE.

You've got some evidence against the professor now. But do you want to deal with this guy directly yourself? Or just forget about it?

WILL YOU...

...keep using the equipment to record their conversation?
TURN TO PAGE 76.

...wait till the van goes through a tunnel, then jump out and escape?
TURN TO PAGE 24.

...scare the driver into pulling over?
TURN TO PAGE 79.

These scientist types turn out to be not so bad. They really go all out to fix you up a place to stay: no windows, nice and cozy.

Plus, they're very polite while they're running all their tests. You like the way the woman in charge thinks. "This is an amazing time to be alive!" she says one day. "For the first time ever, the world is openly accepting not just the existence of vampires, but all of the wonderful things we can learn from your people!"

Turns out vampire blood can be used to make all sorts of medicines and vaccinations and stuff. Which makes sense, you decide, when you think about it. Seriously, when was the last time you had a cold? Like, seven hundred years ago?

It's very different from life all alone back in the castle. But you think you could get used to it.

THE END

OKAY, GRACIELA AND I WILL HEAD BACK INTO THE VILLAGE TO GET THE REST OF THE SUPPLIES.

THAT SOUNDS GOOD.

MARTHA AND JASON AND I WILL EXPLORE THE CASTLE'S GROUNDS BEFORE WE SETTLE IN INSIDE.

THAT'S *IT*. YOU'VE HEARD ENOUGH.

TIME TO PULL THE GLOVES OFF.

TIME TO GET *SERIOUS*.

GO ON TO THE NEXT PAGE.

Looks as if you have a choice,
since the humans are splitting up.

WILL YOU...

...follow Danforth LaTour and the kids
onto the castle grounds?

TURN TO PAGE 106.

...stow away in the van and deal
with the professor and Graciela?

TURN TO PAGE 30.

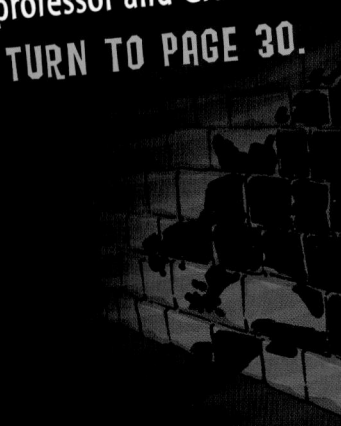

You stay up in the shadows, waiting and watching. You know if you're patient you'll get the perfect opportunity.

It doesn't take long. The professor leads the group into your study. "All right," he says. "We'll make this our base of operations." Danforth brings in a big trunk on wheels, which they open up to reveal an array of guns and a lot of high-tech equipment. You recognize some radios and other communications gear.

Graciela starts sorting all the equipment into two orderly stacks on one of your tables: weapons on one side of the room, communications on the other.

She stays close to the communications gear, fine-tuning a radio.

You're pretty sure you can get to one of those stacks, but not both of them.

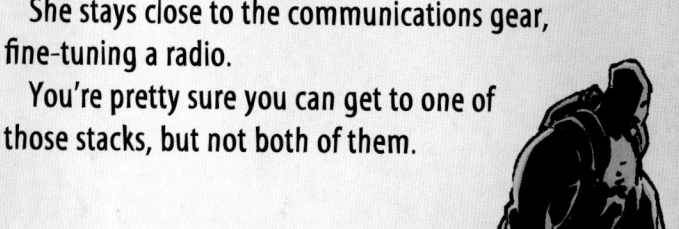

GO ON TO THE NEXT PAGE.

Whatever they're planning to do, you know
you can't let them go through with it.

WILL YOU...

...sabotage their guns?
TURN TO PAGE 87.

...wreck their communications equipment?
TURN TO PAGE 54.

Enough running! It's time to shut this guy down once and for all! And you know just how you'll do it, too. Without even slowing down, you turn and skitter straight up a wall. Then you creep out onto the ceiling and hang there like a great big bug.

Not two seconds later, Focaccia comes running after you and pauses directly below you. "Where'd you go, monster?" he bellows as he looks around.

This is perfect, you think. *I'll just drop right onto his head!*

And drop you do, plummeting down toward the silver-haired vampire hunter—just as he raises the sun gun and points it straight up. "I saw you up there," he murmurs as he pulls the trigger. It's too late to do anything about it. He fires the gun and envelops you in a cone of ultraviolet radiation. Unfortunately for you, that means this is

THE END

The ones running away obviously get the point. You suppose you'll just have to work a little harder on the two teenagers still in the room, since they haven't moved.

You land heavily. Your huge, blood red eyes fix on the girl, and you start dragging yourself across the floor with your wings. You know this is a hideous sight, so you really play it up: *thump, thump, draaaag . . . thump, thump, draaaag . . .* They're going to start running. Any second now. Any second . . .

But instead the girl starts *crying.*

"We're sorry!" she sobs. "We're so sorry! We didn't mean to do anything wrong! Jason and I never even wanted to come here in the first place! Please don't kill us, please don't kill us, *pleeeease . . . !*"

GO ON TO THE NEXT PAGE.

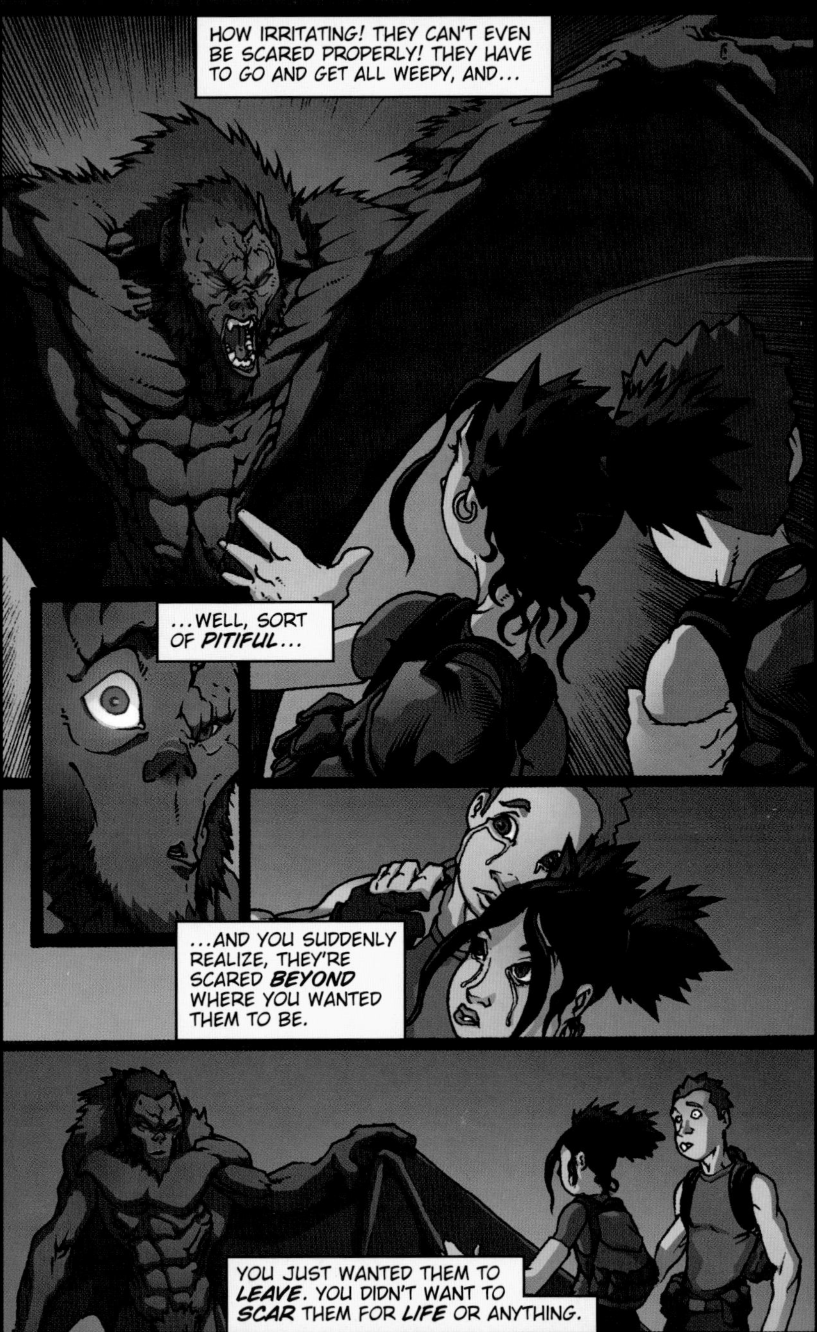
HOW IRRITATING! THEY CAN'T EVEN BE SCARED PROPERLY! THEY HAVE TO GO AND GET ALL WEEPY, AND...
...WELL, SORT OF ***PITIFUL***...
...AND YOU SUDDENLY REALIZE, THEY'RE SCARED ***BEYOND*** WHERE YOU WANTED THEM TO BE.
YOU JUST WANTED THEM TO ***LEAVE***. YOU DIDN'T WANT TO ***SCAR*** THEM FOR ***LIFE*** OR ANYTHING.

GO ON TO THE NEXT PAGE.

You can't believe it, but you really feel
bad for these two kids.

WILL YOU...

... give yourself some time to
think about what to do next?

TURN TO PAGE 53.

... change your shape
enough to speak and
apologize to them?

TURN TO PAGE 56.

The three humans jump when they see you. "Stay back, monster!" Danforth bellows. "Don't come near us!"

"Oh, I won't," you say pleasantly.

"Huh?"

"Because I've already called my uncle. Vampires very rarely call for help, but when they do, everyone knows it's serious."

Suddenly the room grows dark . . . and a pair of glowing red eyes appears in the gloom. They move forward. They belong to a huge, muscular, white-haired man. "Meet Uncle Larry," you say. "He specializes in . . . taking care of problems."

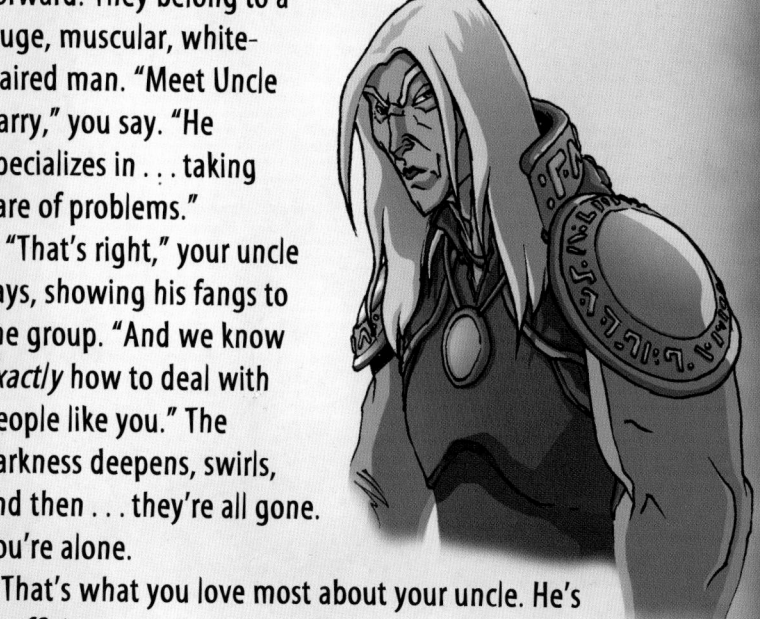

"That's right," your uncle says, showing his fangs to the group. "And we know *exactly* how to deal with people like you." The darkness deepens, swirls, and then . . . they're all gone. You're alone.

That's what you love most about your uncle. He's so *efficient*.

THE END

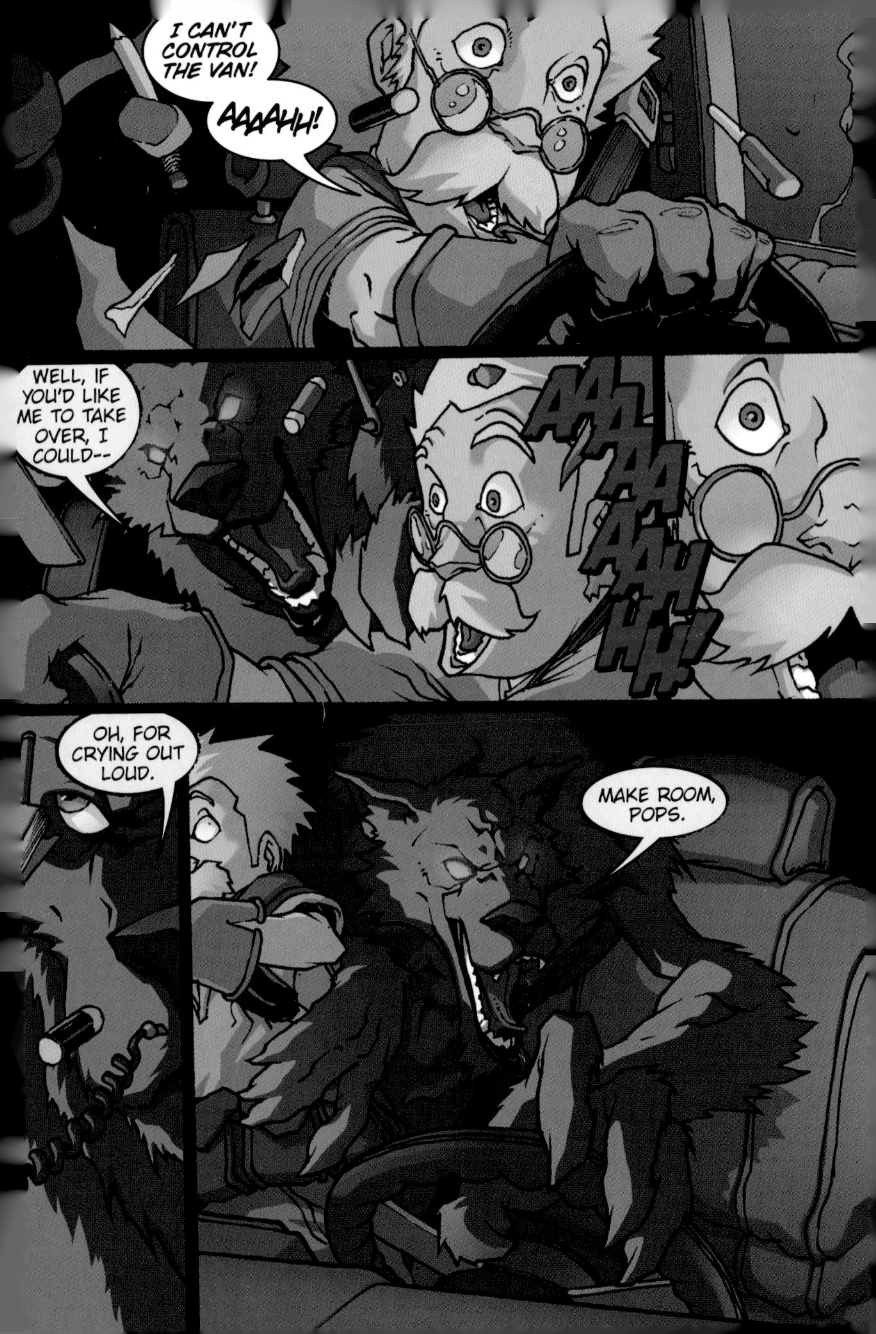
I CAN'T CONTROL THE VAN!
AAAAHH!
WELL, IF YOU'D LIKE ME TO TAKE OVER, I COULD--
AAAAAAAHHH!
OH, FOR CRYING OUT LOUD.
MAKE ROOM, POPS.

It's a close call, but you know this area incredibly well. You get behind the wheel of the van just in time to make it swerve around a house, zip past a small but very loud dog kennel, and come to rest in the parking lot of a bank.

Everything seems eerily silent for a few seconds . . . and then Graciela bursts into tears. "We could've been killed!" she wails. "And you saved us! A vampire saved our lives! This changes *everything*. Is up down? Is black white? I'm going crazy!"

"You're not *that* crazy," you mutter, but you don't think she hears you.

"Calm down," the professor says irritably. "This monster caused the problem in the first place, you know."

Then Professor Gumpert leans toward you. His voice comes out a little quavery. "But she does have a point. You weren't *trying* to kill us. And you *did* save us. Thank you."

"I don't need your thanks," you tell him. "I need you to do three things. First, get it through your head that not all vampires are bad. Second, forget *any* plans you had to turn that boy into a vampire. And third, collect your whole group and *leave*. Go away. Leave me alone and in peace."

He nods somberly. "All right. I see I have a lot to think about anyway. Possibly a lot to reconsider. We'll be on our way at once."

Well. That wasn't *too* hard. All it took to make him see the light of reason was a near-death experience.

Sheesh. *Humans!*

THE END

These humans are the vilest creatures you've
ever encountered. This home has been in
your family for nine hundred fifty years!
You can't let this happen!

WILL YOU...

. . . take care of them on your own?
TURN TO PAGE 55.

. . . call in your uncle, who's a lot
bigger and badder than you are?
TURN TO PAGE 41.

WAIT! WAIT! THERE'S NO NEED FOR VIOLENCE!
HOLD YOUR FIRE, BUT STAY READY. IT'S NOT WISE TO TRUST THE UNDEAD.
AH, BUT THAT'S WHERE YOU'RE WRONG. I AM COMPLETELY TRUSTWORTHY--AS WELL AS FRIENDLY AND HOSPITABLE--
--AS I'LL BE HAPPY TO PROVE TO YOU, IF YOU'LL LOWER YOUR WEAPONS.
DANFORTH? WHAT DO YOU THINK?
I... I DON'T KNOW... NONE OF THEM EVER **SPOKE** TO ME BEFORE...
WELL, I KNOW WHAT *I* THINK.
YOU'VE SEEN ONE VAMPIRE, YOU'VE SEEN 'EM ALL.
YOU SMELL IT A SPLIT SECOND BEFORE IT HITS YOU. IT'S SUPER-CONCENTRATED ***GARLIC ACID!*** AND GARLIC, AS ***EVERYONE*** KNOWS...
...IS ***FATAL*** TO VAMPIRES.
THE END

It only takes you a couple of minutes to zoom down to the sub-basement. You grab a certain bottle filled with a sparkling, silvery powder.

These vampire hunters have got to go, and a friendly young sorceress you met last Halloween showed you a little trick for just such an occasion.

You're moving so fast as you swoop over them that they don't even see you. Not until the dust settles down onto them. Then it only takes a few heartbeats . . .

. . . before Danforth, Jason, and Martha turn to stone.

You've always wanted some decorative statuary. And once the other two get back, you'll have a nice set of five.

THE END

You're too mad to think straight! You just want these creeps out of here as fast as possible, and if that means roughing them up a little bit to help them along, fine. Your leathery wings beat ferociously at the air as you head straight for Danforth's head.

"Look out, Danforth!" Graciela screams. Danforth sees you just in time to duck out of the way. You zoom past him and wheel around. Maybe this time you'll go for his wife.

"That's a vampire!" the man shouts. "It's got to be! Kill it! Kill it!"

To your amazement, every single one of them pulls out some sort of high-tech gun—the sorts of things you'd expect to see in a science-fiction movie.

Hmmm . . . you're not sure what
to make of those guns. Could be dangerous.
Could be nothing to worry about.

WILL YOU...

. . . change to a wolf so you can attack them
with a bigger, more powerful body?

TURN TO PAGE 66.

. . . stay small and fast as a bat and
rely on speed to do the trick?

TURN TO PAGE 88.

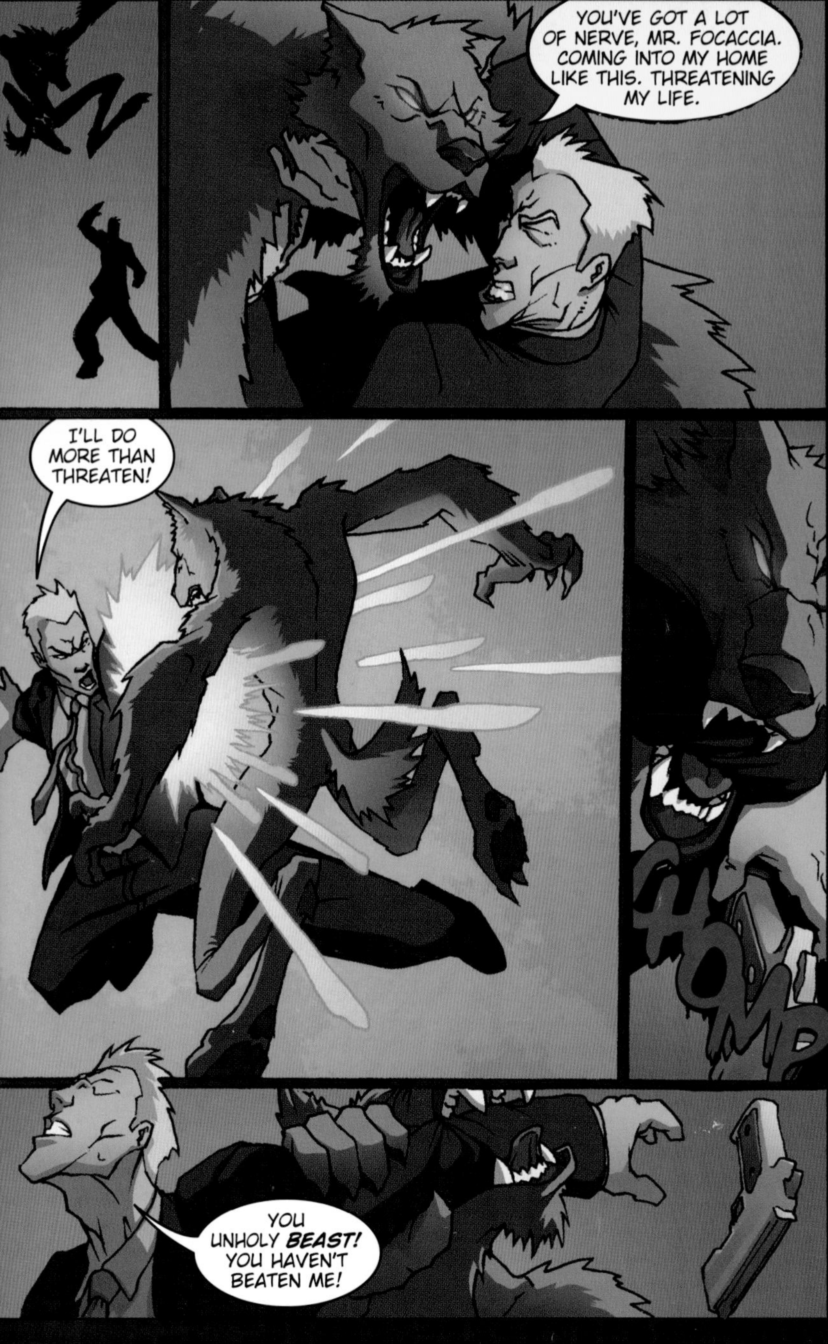
YOU'VE GOT A LOT OF NERVE, MR. FOCACCIA. COMING INTO MY HOME LIKE THIS. THREATENING MY LIFE.
I'LL DO MORE THAN THREATEN!
THOMP
YOU UNHOLY **BEAST!** YOU HAVEN'T BEATEN ME!

GO ON TO THE NEXT PAGE.

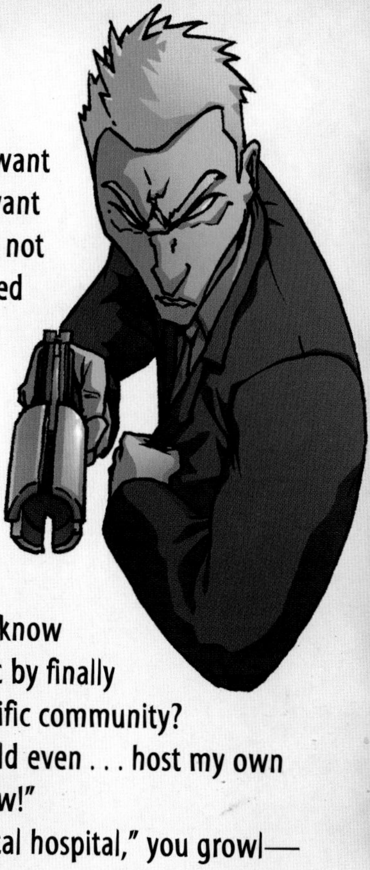

You and Focaccia circle each other slowly. You don't really want to hurt him. You don't really want to hurt *anybody*. But he might not give you a choice if you're forced to defend yourself.

"I've tracked monsters like you my whole life," he says, and his voice comes out high and weird, kind of like a giggle. *Oh yeah*, you say to yourself. *This guy is crazy with a capital* C. "Do you know what kind of recognition I'll get by finally *capturing* one? From the scientific community? From the media? Why . . . I could even . . . host my own late-night horror-movie TV show!"

"Time to go back to the mental hospital," you growl—but then Focaccia yanks something out of his jacket pocket.

"I was saving this for *just* such an occasion," he says. "My new ultraviolet sunlight gun!"

GO ON TO THE NEXT PAGE.

You're pretty sure this guy is a complete whack job . . . but then again, plenty of whack jobs have been dangerous, and if that *sun gun* actually works, you could be in big trouble.

WILL YOU...

. . . rush in and knock this guy's block off?

TURN TO PAGE 98.

. . . decide "discretion is the better part of valor" and get out of there?

TURN TO PAGE 62.

Staring into their eyes, you let the power of your mind flow into Martha and Jason. "The world goes away now," you whisper.

"The world goes away," they both repeat in unison. Then their eyes close as they freeze in place, rigid as statues. They'll stay that way—quiet and out of your hair—until you release them.

From elsewhere in the castle you hear a familiar sound, followed by a terrified shriek. Sounds like the grown-ups found the trapdoor to the oubliette, your special dungeon pit with no doors or windows. How about that?

Of course, you'll have to fish out Graciela and Danforth pretty quickly, since they haven't done anything wrong. The professor . . . might just stay there at the bottom of the well for a while.

All these humans. What to do with them? Freeze the parents too, of course.

You'll decide what their fates will be after a nap.

A very, very *long* nap.

THE END

53

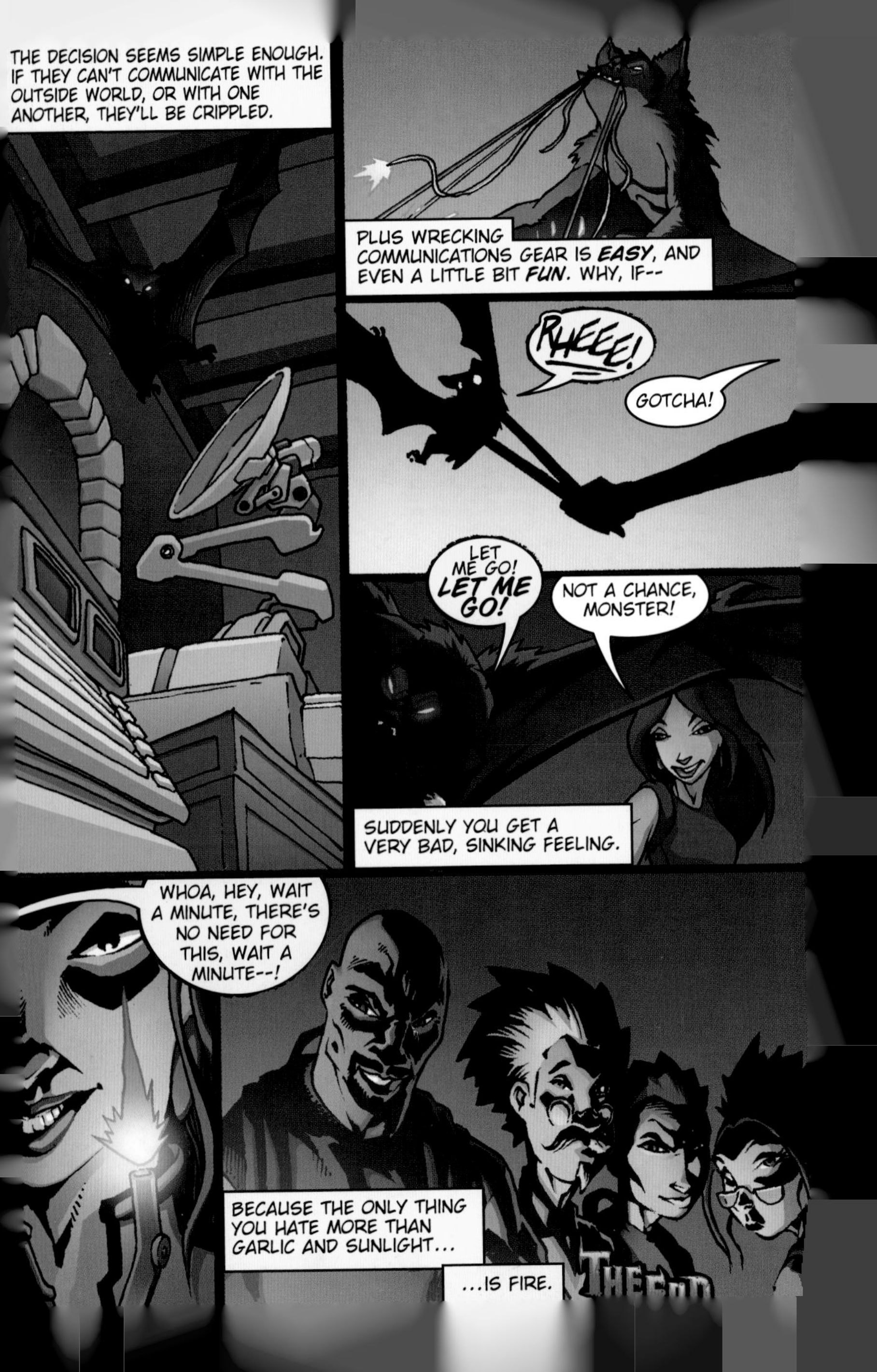
THE DECISION SEEMS SIMPLE ENOUGH. IF THEY CAN'T COMMUNICATE WITH THE OUTSIDE WORLD, OR WITH ONE ANOTHER, THEY'LL BE CRIPPLED.
PLUS WRECKING COMMUNICATIONS GEAR IS ***EASY***, AND EVEN A LITTLE BIT ***FUN***. WHY, IF--
RHEEEE!
GOTCHA!
LET ME GO! ***LET ME GO!***
NOT A CHANCE, MONSTER!
SUDDENLY YOU GET A VERY BAD, SINKING FEELING.
WHOA, HEY, WAIT A MINUTE, THERE'S NO NEED FOR THIS, WAIT A MINUTE--!
BECAUSE THE ONLY THING YOU HATE MORE THAN GARLIC AND SUNLIGHT...
...IS FIRE.

You step out from the shadows, your fangs visible. "I was going to come back here and warn you people," you growl. "But now I've got a better idea."

They try to run, but you're much too fast for them. Once they're all unconscious, you drag them back into the library and . . . well, "bite" is such an indelicate word. Let's just say you make sure they won't threaten your home anymore.

They're pretty freaked out when they wake up again. "You monster!" the father shouts. "You've turned us into *vampires?*"

"Hey, don't knock it," you reply. "It's not a bad life. Plus, I'd love to see you mistreat our kind now."

Ha! They've got no answer for *that!* Serves 'em right anyway.

Now . . . only thing left is to track down the other two, and you can call it a night.

Not a problem.

THE END

You're surprised to realize that not only do you believe Martha, you also feel genuinely guilty for frightening her and Jason so badly.

Swiftly you change back into a much more human form.

"Hey, listen," you say to them. "I'm sorry. I know you guys didn't know what was going on here. I shouldn't have gone after you like I did."

"Wh-what do you mean?" the girl stammers. "What's going on here?"

You tell them everything you heard about the professor's intention to turn Jason into a vampire and then study him. They're both shocked.

While they're dealing with it, you hear a familiar sound from somewhere in the castle: The adults have just slid down a trapdoor ramp into your dungeon. That's fine—you can deal with them later.

With the adults temporarily taken care of
and the teenagers feeling more comfortable
with you, what happens now?

WILL YOU...

...invite the teenagers to join
you for dinner?
TURN TO PAGE 90.

...send them on their way?
TURN TO PAGE 102.

You take a step toward the boy. He gasps and takes a step back. Your lips peel away from your teeth as you give him your best menacing snarl.

He probably wouldn't be this scared if he knew how long I practiced that snarl in front of a mirror.

That's another thing about vampires that most people don't know. You can see *yourself* in a mirror just fine. It's only humans who see no reflection.

Finally, the kid catches his breath enough to whisper, "Please . . . don't hurt me! I don't wanna die!"

You feel like snorting. As if you'd really bite a human! You used to *be* one, after all.

GO ON TO THE NEXT PAGE.

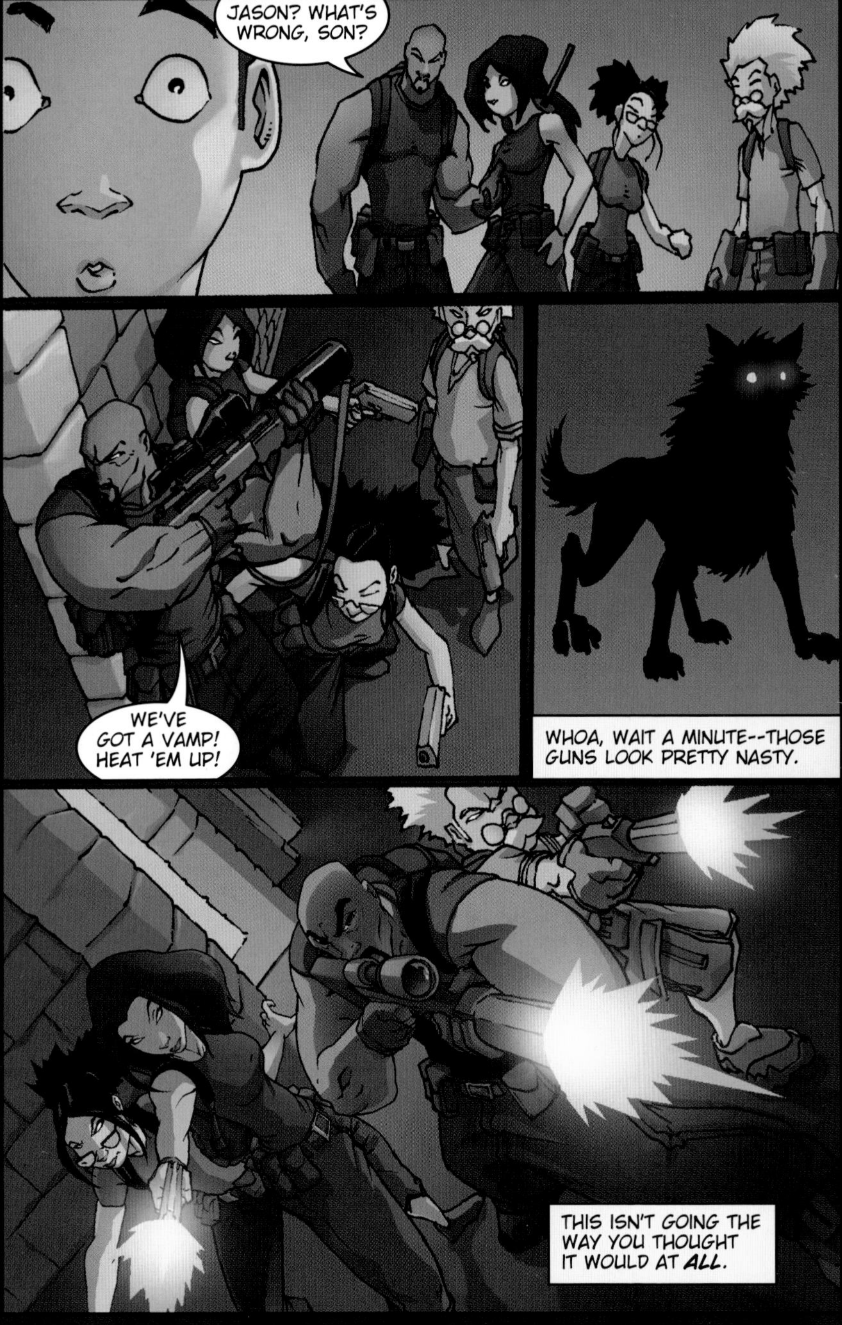
JASON? WHAT'S WRONG, SON?
WE'VE GOT A VAMP! HEAT 'EM UP!
WHOA, WAIT A MINUTE--THOSE GUNS LOOK PRETTY NASTY.
THIS ISN'T GOING THE WAY YOU THOUGHT IT WOULD AT ***ALL***.

GO ON TO THE NEXT PAGE.

You've never dealt with vampire hunters who had guns like these. But then again, they *are* just humans. You could probably beat them if you wanted to.

WILL YOU...

...stand your ground and fight?

TURN TO PAGE 26.

...get away from there so you can regroup and decide what to do?

TURN TO PAGE 65.

...try to be rational and explain that there's no reason for any violence?

TURN TO PAGE 46.

Ugh. *Werewolves.* You can't stand werewolves! They multiply like cockroaches and they're twice as annoying. You have to get rid of this kid before he decides to make your castle into his new den.

So you turn solid again and glide forward, straight toward him. You figure if you can tackle him, you can lock him in your dungeon until you figure out the best course of action.

But then he turns and sees you coming—and you've never seen a werewolf transform so quickly . . . or get so *big.* All of a sudden, it's the werewolf picking *you* up instead of the other way around, and you have just enough time to realize you've made a really serious strategic error . . .

. . . and then his jaws chomp down on your head, and that's . . .

THE END

"Y'know, I think I'll have to catch up with you some other time," you mutter as you spin on one paw and bolt toward the door. The family has already disappeared into the castle somewhere. It's just yourself you have to worry about now . . .

. . . but then you hear a strange whining sound, followed by a flash of light like a small supernova. Suddenly you feel intense burning pain along your right flank.

"Ha!" Focaccia shouts. "Got you! I got you! How's pure sunlight feel, vampire? Stings a little, does it? Hmmmmm?"

He's right, he tagged you solidly. You know it'll take days for the burn to heal. But you can't think about that right now. First things first: Get away from this guy before he burns off your head!

GO ON TO THE NEXT PAGE.

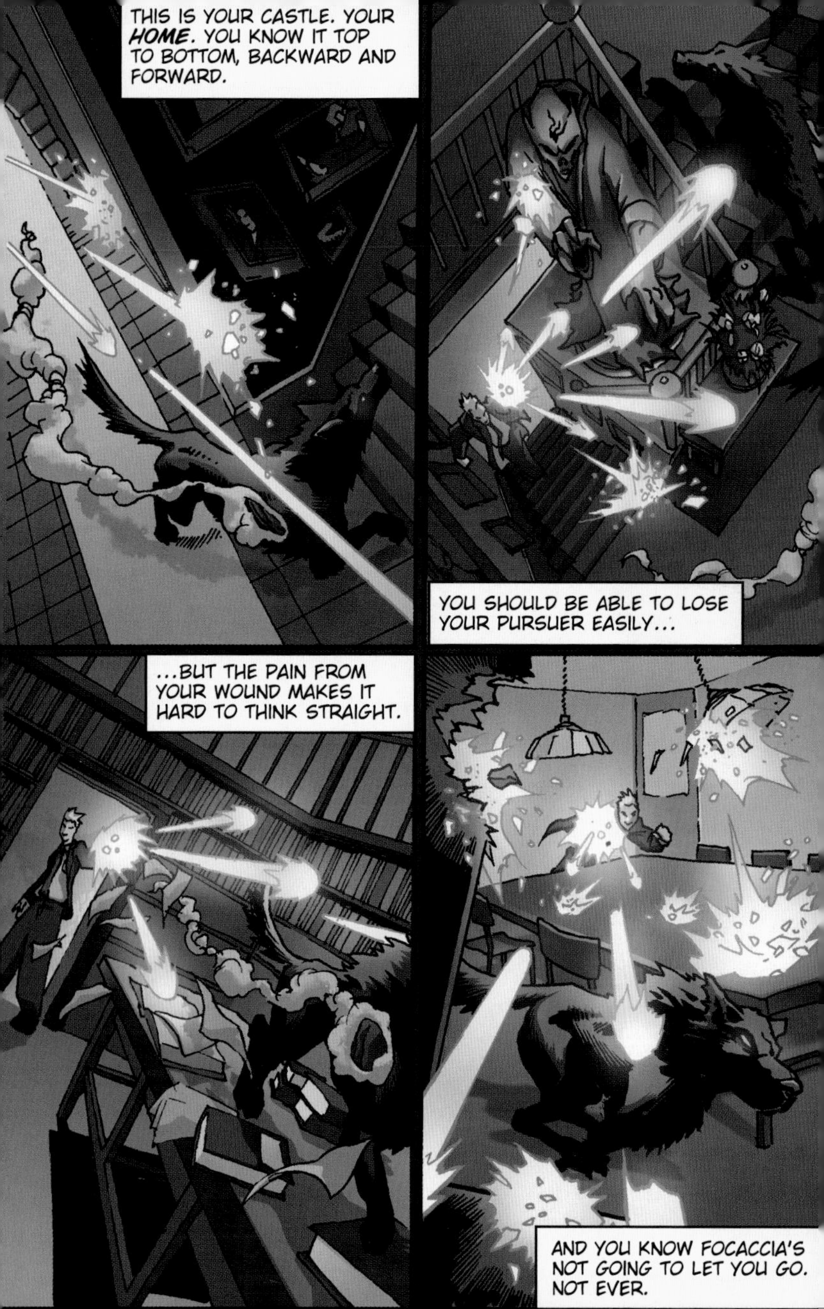
THIS IS YOUR CASTLE. YOUR *HOME*. YOU KNOW IT TOP TO BOTTOM, BACKWARD AND FORWARD.
YOU SHOULD BE ABLE TO LOSE YOUR PURSUER EASILY...
...BUT THE PAIN FROM YOUR WOUND MAKES IT HARD TO THINK STRAIGHT.
AND YOU KNOW FOCACCIA'S NOT GOING TO LET YOU GO. NOT EVER.

It's time to act, *right now*.
But what are you going to do?

WILL YOU...

... make a stand here and confront him directly?

TURN TO PAGE 37.

... lure him into the dungeon
and see if you can trap him there?

TURN TO PAGE 17.

... rely on your vampire cunning
and try to trick him?

TURN TO PAGE 103.

... forget all about this "playing nice" stuff
and just turn him into a vampire?

TURN TO PAGE 104.

Guns can't hurt vampires ... but there's something about *these* guns you don't like. You whip around and sprint away from them, heading back toward the stairs ...

... but suddenly a net made of metal mesh wraps tightly around you.

"As if a net's going to hold me," you growl through wolfish teeth. "I'll turn into something tiny and slip away!"

But the professor comes and kneels down next to you. He doesn't seem the tiniest bit afraid. "Sorry, but you won't be going anywhere," he says smugly. "I've been developing this Neuro-Neutralizer Net for *decades*. Its phrenotic pulses have your brain locked up *tight*. You're stuck in wolf form as long as you're tangled in it. And now ... I'm taking you back to my laboratory. For some experimentation."

He's right. You can't change. You can't even move.

"Pack it up," he tells the others. "We're done here!"

THE END

The humans back away from you as you start to change again. They're not scared. *Yet.*

"Don't be alarmed!" the professor says from the doorway. "It's changing from a bat into a wolf! We can kill a wolf!"

But you can see that confidence start to fade as your body grows long and lean—and keeps growing. You're changing into a wolf, all right. A wolf the size of a small *car.*

"Get . . . *out,*" you growl. Your voice is so deep and loud it makes the stone floor vibrate.

You're not sure, but you think Danforth might have just wet his pants.

Then they're all screaming and running. You stop at the door and watch as they jump into their van and peel out. The van's wheels spray rocks and earth behind them as they leave. You know people pretty well . . . and you don't think they'll be back.

That was fun!

THE END

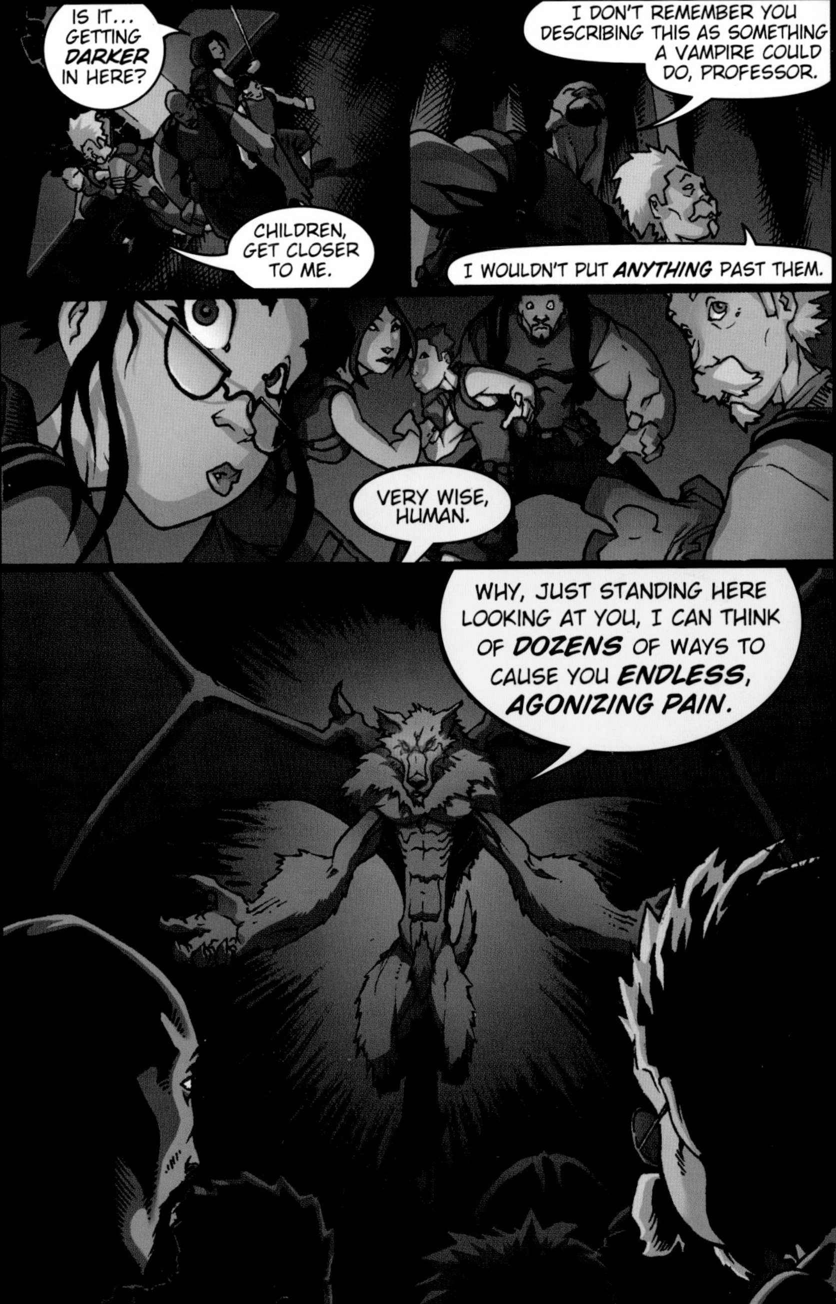
IS IT... GETTING **DARKER** IN HERE?
CHILDREN, GET CLOSER TO ME.
I DON'T REMEMBER YOU DESCRIBING THIS AS SOMETHING A VAMPIRE COULD DO, PROFESSOR.
I WOULDN'T PUT **ANYTHING** PAST THEM.
VERY WISE, HUMAN.
WHY, JUST STANDING HERE LOOKING AT YOU, I CAN THINK OF **DOZENS** OF WAYS TO CAUSE YOU **ENDLESS, AGONIZING PAIN.**

GO ON TO THE NEXT PAGE.

You're proud of yourself for how scary that sounded. You'll have to tell your cousin Marcy about this. And it *worked!* Every one of them turns tail and runs back toward the main entrance. "I never knew they could look like *that!*" the professor screams. "We have to get out of here!"

You follow along, out of sight again in the darkness, just to make sure they're really leaving. And you're glad you did, because the teenage boy slows down and stops. He turns and looks around—straight at you! Can he see you there in the shadows?

"I'm not sure if you're there," the boy says softly. None of the others hears him. "But I'm sorry I got so scared. I don't really think you mean to hurt anybody. Maybe later I can come back alone, and we can talk."

Once again, you're amazed. This kid has guts!

This is clearly a good kid. And he can tell that you're good too. But still, good kids don't have any reason to go looking for trouble the way he and his family have.

WILL YOU...

. . . reinforce the scare by snapping at him?
TURN TO PAGE 78.

. . . drop the scary act and reassure him kindly?
TURN TO PAGE 91.

MOM, DAD! LOOK!

THIS MIGHT BE TRICKY. THEIR NATURAL FIRST REACTION WILL PROBABLY EITHER BE TO RUN AWAY OR TRY TO KILL YOU.

I--AHEM-- I DON'T KNOW IF YOU CAN UNDERSTAND ME... BUT WE'RE NOT HERE TO HURT YOU. WE DON'T MEAN YOU ANY HARM.

OF COURSE I CAN UNDERSTAND YOU. I SPEAK ENGLISH JUST AS WELL AS YOU.

AND I HOPE YOU'RE SINCERE WHEN YOU SAY YOU MEAN ME NO HARM, BECAUSE THE FEELING IS VERY MUCH MUTUAL.

THEY WEREN'T EXPECTING *THAT!* YOU HAVE TO WORK HARD NOT TO GIGGLE AT HOW SILLY THEY ALL LOOK.

GO ON TO THE NEXT PAGE.

The professor steps forward timidly. "You—you mean—oh, I can't believe I'm talking to you—this is so exciting! *Ahem.* Do you mean that you're truly not intending to do us any harm? You don't want to . . . drink our blood, per se?"

"Good heavens, no!" you splutter. "There are plenty of good substitutes on the market, if you know where to shop. I order all of mine off the Internet."

His eyes light up with eagerness. "Then you'll talk with us?"

"Yes, I will," you reply, "but for one reason and one reason alone. I'm tired of the way movies and TV shows make vampires look. We're just hardworking people like anybody else."

TURN TO PAGE 94.

You watch as the humans bring in a big trunk and start setting up some kind of base of operations in your study. They 're pretty businesslike . . . except for Professor Gumpert. He keeps sneaking glances over at the others, like he's up to something. When he leaves the room, you decide to follow him.

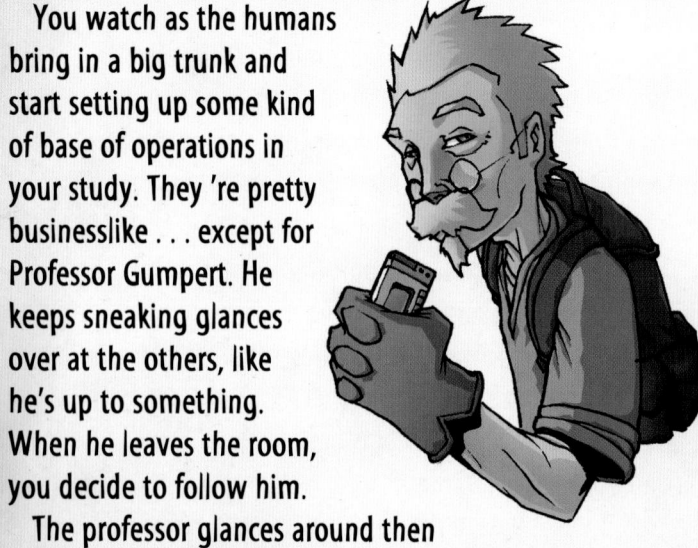

The professor glances around then talks into his little handheld recorder. With your bat ears, you can hear him whispering as clearly as if he were shouting.

"My plan has worked flawlessly so far. If my findings are correct, I should be able to isolate young Jason with the vampire before the night is over. He'll be bitten, and then I can take him back to my laboratory—as my very own vampire test subject."

He's going to . . . *what?* Is this guy *serious?*

GO ON TO THE NEXT PAGE.

YOU'VE HEARD AND SEEN SOME AWFUL, TERRIBLE THINGS IN YOUR DAY. BUT THIS TAKES THE CAKE.

HOW'RE YOU DOING, PROFESSOR? HOLDING UP ALL RIGHT? NOT TOO TIRED AFTER THE LONG DRIVE?

NO, NO, I'M FINE, I'M FINE! JUST HAPPY TO BE HERE. ESPECIALLY WHEN I GET TO WORK WITH SUCH ENTHUSIASTIC YOUNG PEOPLE!

BECOMING A VAMPIRE IS A BIG DEAL...A HUGE, SERIOUS, *PERMANENT* DEAL.

AND TO TRY TO FORCE IT ON SOMEONE? THAT'S JUST *LOW*.

THE KID'S LUCKY THEY'RE HERE. YOU'RE CERTAINLY NOT GOING TO BITE HIM, BUT YOU KNOW PLENTY OF OTHER VAMPIRES WHO *WOULD*.

IN ANY CASE, THERE IS *NO WAY* YOU'RE GOING TO LET THE PROFESSOR GO AHEAD WITH THIS HORRIBLE PLAN.

GO ON TO THE NEXT PAGE.

73

You're so angry you can barely see straight.
The professor can't be allowed to do what he's
planning. But exactly *how* will you stop him?

WILL YOU...

. . . confront the humans directly
and simply tell them?

TURN TO PAGE 80.

. . . attack and drive them all out?

TURN TO PAGE 100.

. . . put aside your reasonable nature
and get *really* serious?

TURN TO PAGE 33.

"Now, listen," you tell the humans. "It's better than being a werewolf, but being a vampire isn't easy. There are a lot of limits and dangers to get used to."

"Will I be in control of myself?" Jason asks. "Will I stop turning into a beast and going on uncontrolled rampages?"

"Well...yes."

"Then sign me up."

While Danforth and Martha watch anxiously, you step forward and bite the boy on his outstretched wrist. "How long does it take?" Jason asks.

"Three days or so," you tell him.

"Listen," Danforth says, "you obviously know all about this. Could we stay here for a while? With you? Get you to explain things for us?"

It only takes you a few seconds to think it over. "Sure," you tell him. "I'll get the spare bedrooms ready. Come on, follow me."

You've always been a sucker for vampire-in-distress stories.

THE END

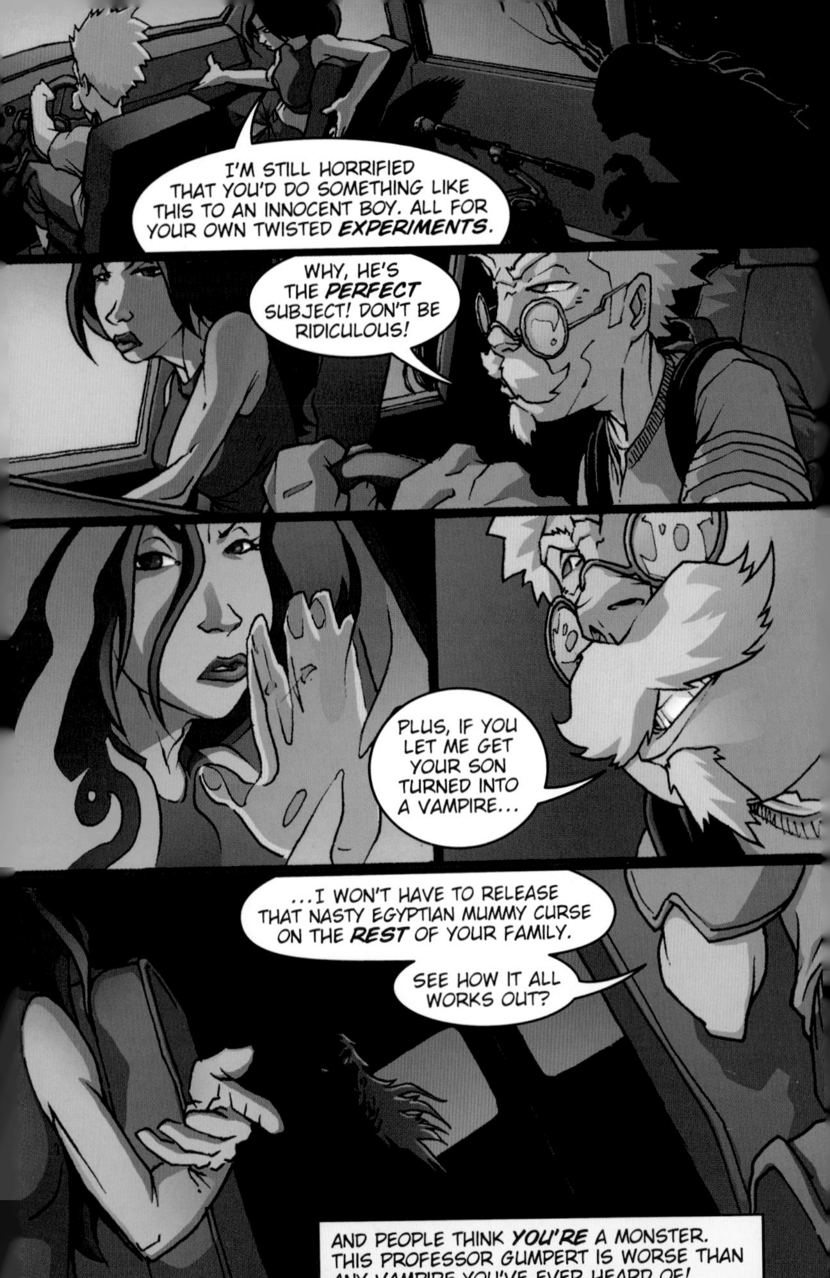
I'M STILL HORRIFIED THAT YOU'D DO SOMETHING LIKE THIS TO AN INNOCENT BOY. ALL FOR YOUR OWN TWISTED ***EXPERIMENTS***.
WHY, HE'S THE ***PERFECT*** SUBJECT! DON'T BE RIDICULOUS!
PLUS, IF YOU LET ME GET YOUR SON TURNED INTO A VAMPIRE...
...I WON'T HAVE TO RELEASE THAT NASTY EGYPTIAN MUMMY CURSE ON THE ***REST*** OF YOUR FAMILY.
SEE HOW IT ALL WORKS OUT?
AND PEOPLE THINK ***YOU'RE*** A MONSTER. THIS PROFESSOR GUMPERT IS WORSE THAN ANY VAMPIRE YOU'VE EVER HEARD OF!

After escaping from the van with the recorder, it's no trouble hiding out until nightfall. Then it's a matter of getting to the nearest town. You've just got to get this information out to the public.

You finally find a small police station. This late at night you're afraid no one will be there . . . but there's one light burning.

The one officer on duty almost has a heart attack when he sees you, but he stays calm long enough to hear what you have to say. "Play this recording," you tell him and give him the names of everyone involved.

"Ah-ah-ah-all right," the man says. You watch as he hits PLAY.

TURN TO PAGE 29.

You know what he's trying to do. It seems like in every one of the vampire-hunter groups you've encountered, there's always one guy who thinks he can "connect" with the vampire. Even communicate in one way or another. He's trying to be your friend.

Right now, you can't be his friend, though. He needs to get out of this business before he ends up getting hurt. You rumble out your best growl yet . . . then rush forward and snap at him. Your teeth clack together about an inch from his nose.

The boy screams and runs so fast he's a blur.

It's for the best. You know it is. This way he'll leave and go home and maybe stay safe.

Some other vampires aren't so easygoing about this kind of thing.

THE END

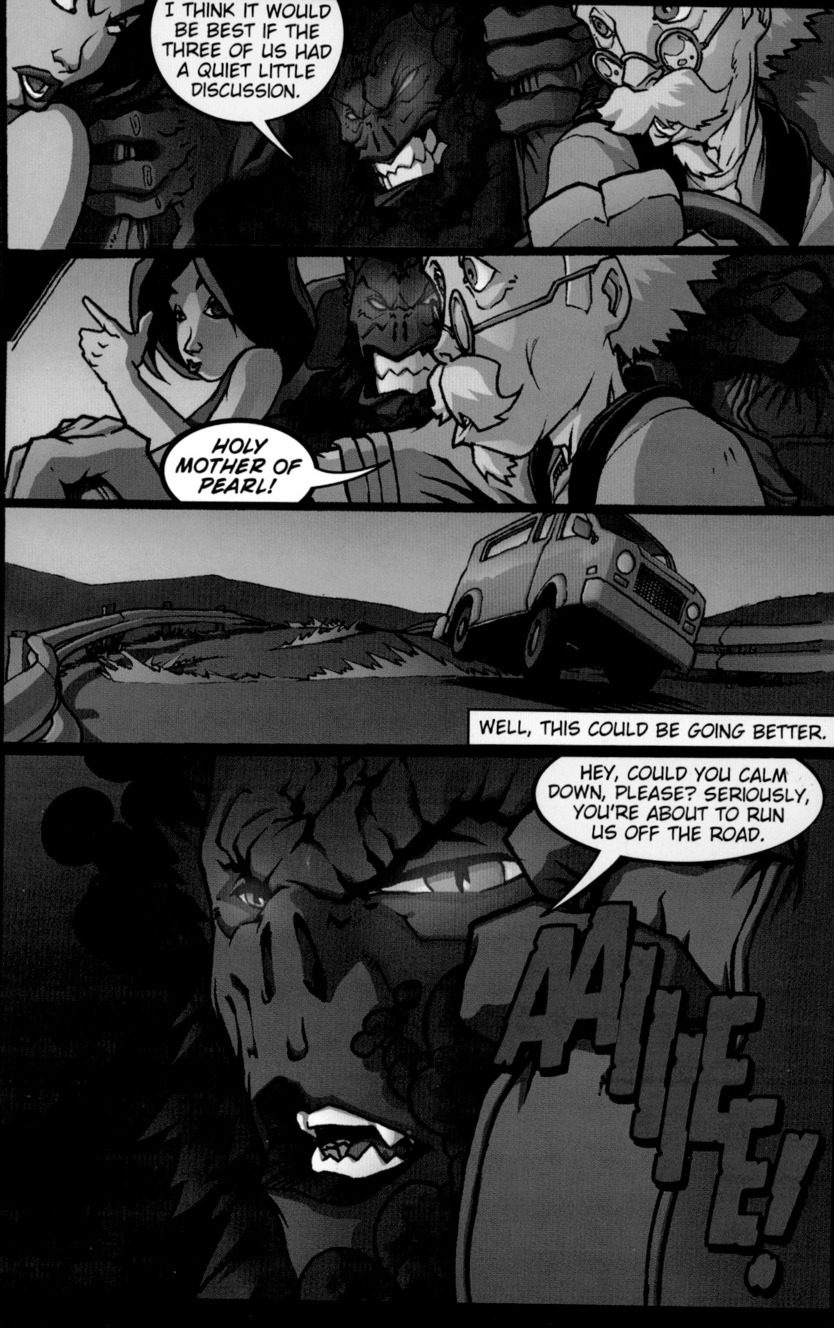
I THINK IT WOULD BE BEST IF THE THREE OF US HAD A QUIET LITTLE DISCUSSION.
HOLY MOTHER OF PEARL!
WELL, THIS COULD BE GOING BETTER.
HEY, COULD YOU CALM DOWN, PLEASE? SERIOUSLY, YOU'RE ABOUT TO RUN US OFF THE ROAD.
AAIIEE!

TURN TO PAGE 83.

While the professor is still out in the hall, you swoop into the room and change back to a shape that looks a little more human. "You have to listen to me," you tell them. "That man you're working with is planning something horrible." And you tell them everything you've heard.

They believe you—once they get over their initial shock. Jason in particular is stunned. "He was going to try to turn me into a vampire? Just so he could *study* me?"

Things move quickly after that. The group confronts the professor, who can't deny his scheme—after they play the recording. He ends up locked in the van while the rest of the humans decide what to do with him.

"We're so grateful to you," Graciela tells you. "Listen . . . would you like to come with us? Back to America?"

Go with them? Go to *America?* You've always been curious about that place...and it would be fun to visit Cousin Marcy. But this is your *home!*

WILL YOU...

...take them up on their offer and travel with them?

TURN TO PAGE 85.

...be more practical and stay here in the castle?

TURN TO PAGE 105.

You turn "human" again. In under five seconds, you're looking the kid in the eye, back on his level.

"Look, I understand that you're a nice, intelligent guy," you say gently. "But you're not cut out for this. What would be best for both of us is if you got rid of this whole vampire-investigation thing and just went home. Where it's nice and safe."

The boy grins a little sheepishly at you. "Yeah," he says. "Yeah, you're probably right. Well . . . sorry to disturb you. I'll make sure my family leaves you alone."

"I appreciate that," you tell him. He gives you a smile and a wave, then runs off to join his people.

You fade back into the shadows as you hear the van start up and begin moving away.
Nice kid, you say to yourself. *But I'm glad I'm back in the peace and quiet now.*

THE END

The professor's having some sort of fit, and the van's going completely out of control!

WILL YOU...

...stay in the van and ride out the crash?
TURN TO PAGE 92.

...jump out and take your chances?
TURN TO PAGE 22.

...try to get behind the wheel and take control of the van?
TURN TO PAGE 42.

"Anti-werewolf serum? I've never heard of that," the boy says suspiciously.

"I brew it myself. It's more definite than biting you, but . . . there could be some . . . unexpected side effects."

The kid's face brightens. "Who cares? Give me the serum!"

You lead them down to your basement laboratory and get to work. A few hours later, you hand him a small bottle. "Drink it all at once," you tell him.

He does. "Wow," he says when he's finished. "It worked! I can feel it! I'm not a werewolf anymore!"

His sister gasps. "Check out your teeth!"

Jason opens his mouth—and carefully touches the long, pointed fangs there with the tip of his tongue. "Hey, y'know what? I like 'em! Thank you! Thank you so much!"

"Happy to help," you tell him.

The boy and his family leave, gladly promising never to return. All in all, not a bad day's work.

THE END

THE OFFER THE HUMANS MADE YOU WAS JUST TOO GOOD TO PASS UP.

BEFORE YOU KNOW IT, YOU'RE PACKED UP AND FLYING FIRST CLASS. SO TO SPEAK.

ALL YOU *REALLY* WANT TO DO IS SEE THE SIGHTS.

BUT THERE ARE A LOT OF PEOPLE WHO WANT TO TALK TO YOU. NOT ONLY FROM HOLLYWOOD...

...BUT ALSO FROM THE BEST AMERICAN SCIENTIFIC LABORATORIES.

BOTH GROUPS SAY THEY CAN MAKE YOU INCREDIBLY FAMOUS.

GO ON TO THE NEXT PAGE.

Well, now that you're here, you figure you might as well go the distance. But what group do you stick with?

WILL YOU...

...go with the scientists, so you can advance the world's academic knowledge?

TURN TO PAGE 32.

...go with the movie and TV producers, so you can become a big-shot celebrity?

TURN TO PAGE 109.

When a vampire decides to be sneaky, there's nothing sneakier on *Earth*. You land next to the biggest of the weapons.

You lick your lips . . . then a few quick, well-placed chomps and the guns are just a bunch of scrap metal. You're already back in the shadows, watching, before the humans even realize what the chomping noise was.

One of the teenagers notices first. "Uh . . . Professor? What happened to the guns?"

The professor comes over. When he sees what you've done, his face turns a strange shade of gray. His fear quickly infects the rest of the humans.

"The vampire did that . . . while we were *in the room!*" Graciela says, her voice shaking. "We're not prepared for this! Let's get out of here!"

They don't even take their equipment. They just run out the front door. Obviously they never learned an important lesson:

Don't bring guns to a bat fight.

THE END

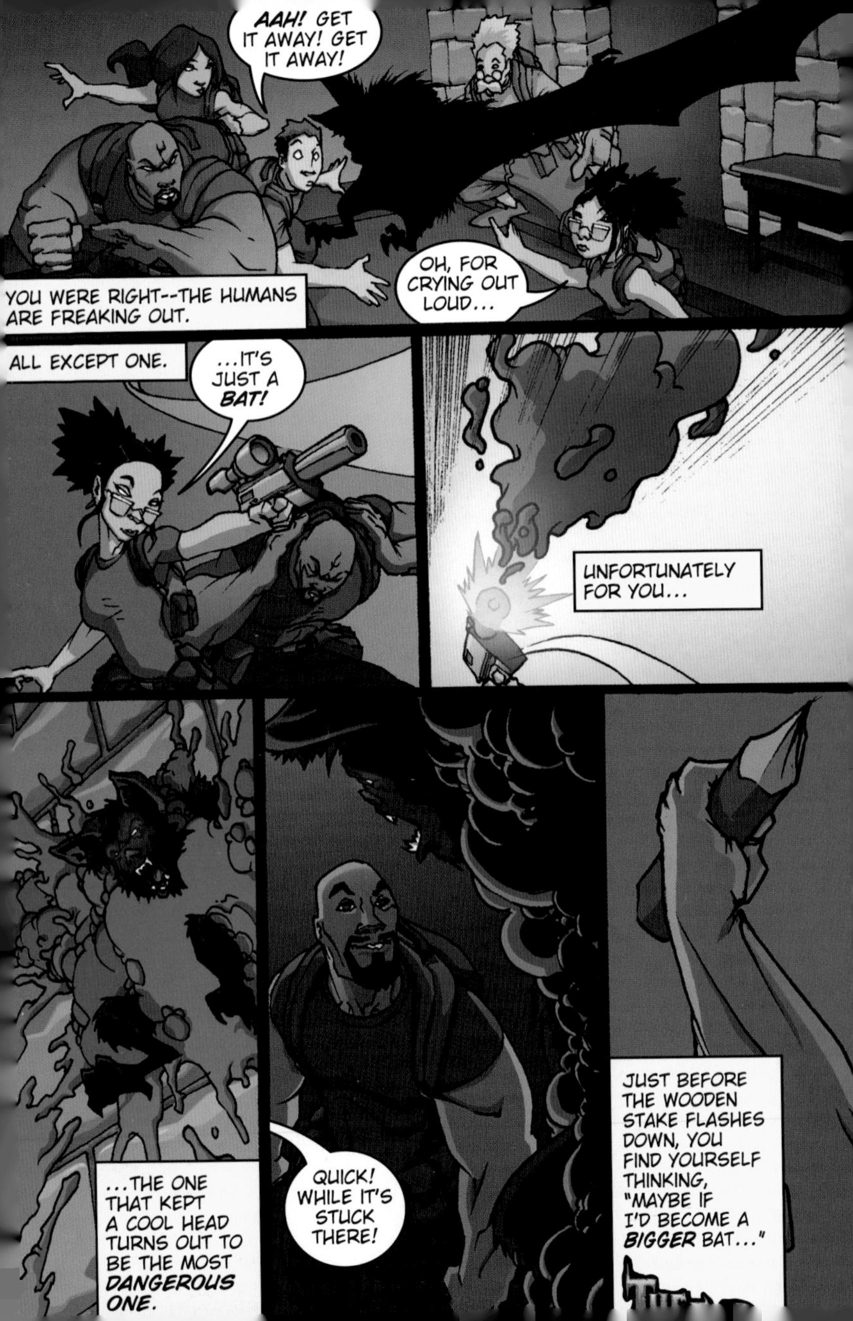

AAH! GET IT AWAY! GET IT AWAY!
YOU WERE RIGHT--THE HUMANS ARE FREAKING OUT.
OH, FOR CRYING OUT LOUD...
ALL EXCEPT ONE.
...IT'S JUST A BAT!
UNFORTUNATELY FOR YOU...
...THE ONE THAT KEPT A COOL HEAD TURNS OUT TO BE THE MOST DANGEROUS ONE.
QUICK! WHILE IT'S STUCK THERE!
JUST BEFORE THE WOODEN STAKE FLASHES DOWN, YOU FIND YOURSELF THINKING, "MAYBE IF I'D BECOME A BIGGER BAT..."

You rush past the shrieking, paralyzed teenagers and shoot down the hallway after the adults. Your snarling echoes up and down the corridor as the tips of your wings almost brush the walls on both sides. Soon you catch sight of them, rounding the corner toward the kitchen.

"How do we get out of here?" Danforth shouts. "I'm completely lost!"

"Just come along!" the professor snaps. "I know the way! Follow me!"

He knows the way, you say to yourself sarcastically. *There's no exit from the kitchen! It just leads to more rooms in the center of the castle!*

A ferocious growl builds in your throat as you turn sharply and swoop after the humans.

TURN TO PAGE 96.

"I feel just awful about this," you say to the kids. "It isn't your fault, but you're stuck in a terrible situation. Why don't you join me for dinner, and we can decide together where to go from here?"

"I, uh, don't mean to be rude," the boy murmurs, "but aren't you a *vampire?* Don't you eat . . . well . . . blood?
We can't, uh, we can't eat blood."

"Relax. I do a stroganoff dish that'll make your toes curl. Come on, follow me."

They do follow, very reluctantly. As you lead them to the kitchen, the girl asks, "What about our parents? And the professor?"

"Well, I'm pretty sure your parents didn't know about the professor's plan. So I'll let them go after I give them a stern talking to. The professor . . . well, he's dangerous. I might keep him a while longer."

GO ON TO THE NEXT PAGE.

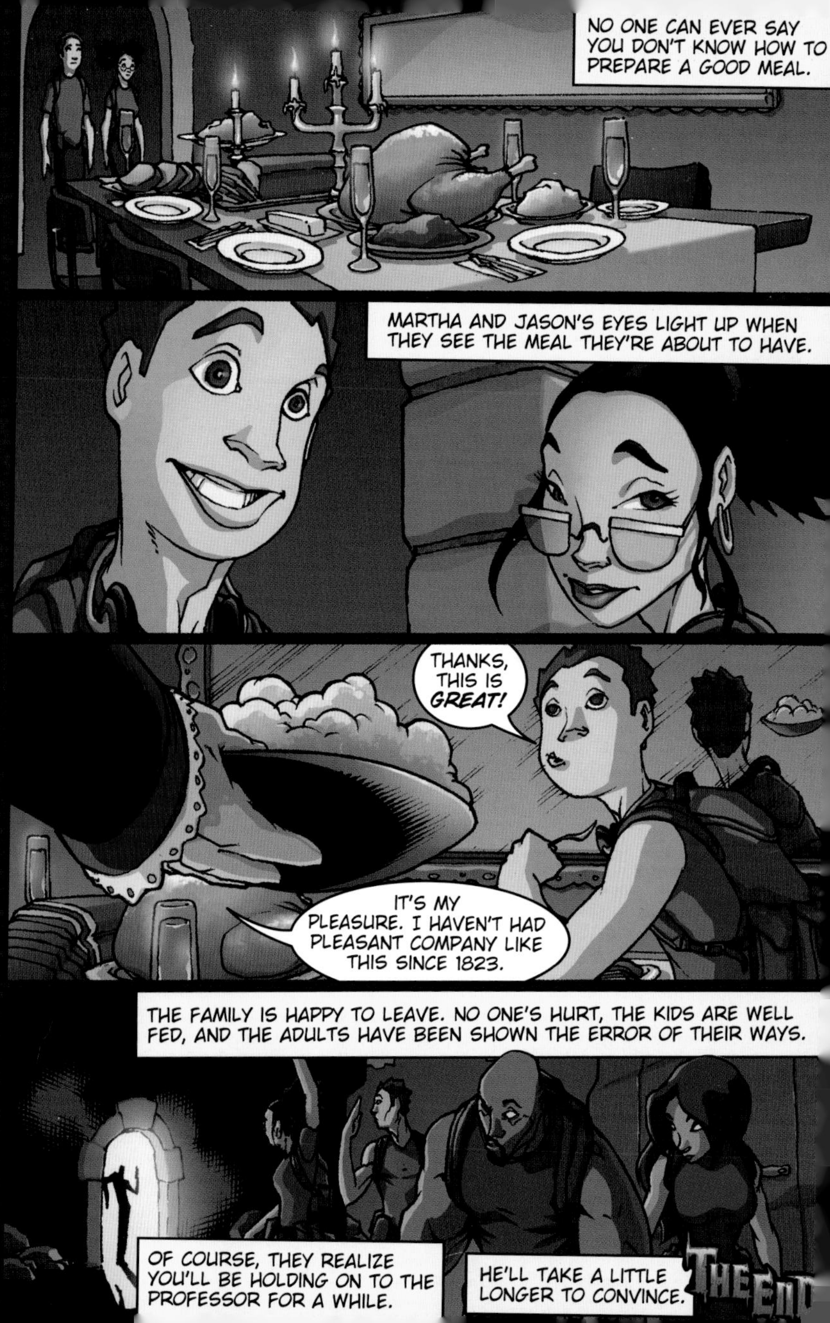
NO ONE CAN EVER SAY YOU DON'T KNOW HOW TO PREPARE A GOOD MEAL.
MARTHA AND JASON'S EYES LIGHT UP WHEN THEY SEE THE MEAL THEY'RE ABOUT TO HAVE.
THANKS, THIS IS *GREAT!*
IT'S MY PLEASURE. I HAVEN'T HAD PLEASANT COMPANY LIKE THIS SINCE 1823.
THE FAMILY IS HAPPY TO LEAVE. NO ONE'S HURT, THE KIDS ARE WELL FED, AND THE ADULTS HAVE BEEN SHOWN THE ERROR OF THEIR WAYS.
OF COURSE, THEY REALIZE YOU'LL BE HOLDING ON TO THE PROFESSOR FOR A WHILE.
HE'LL TAKE A LITTLE LONGER TO CONVINCE.

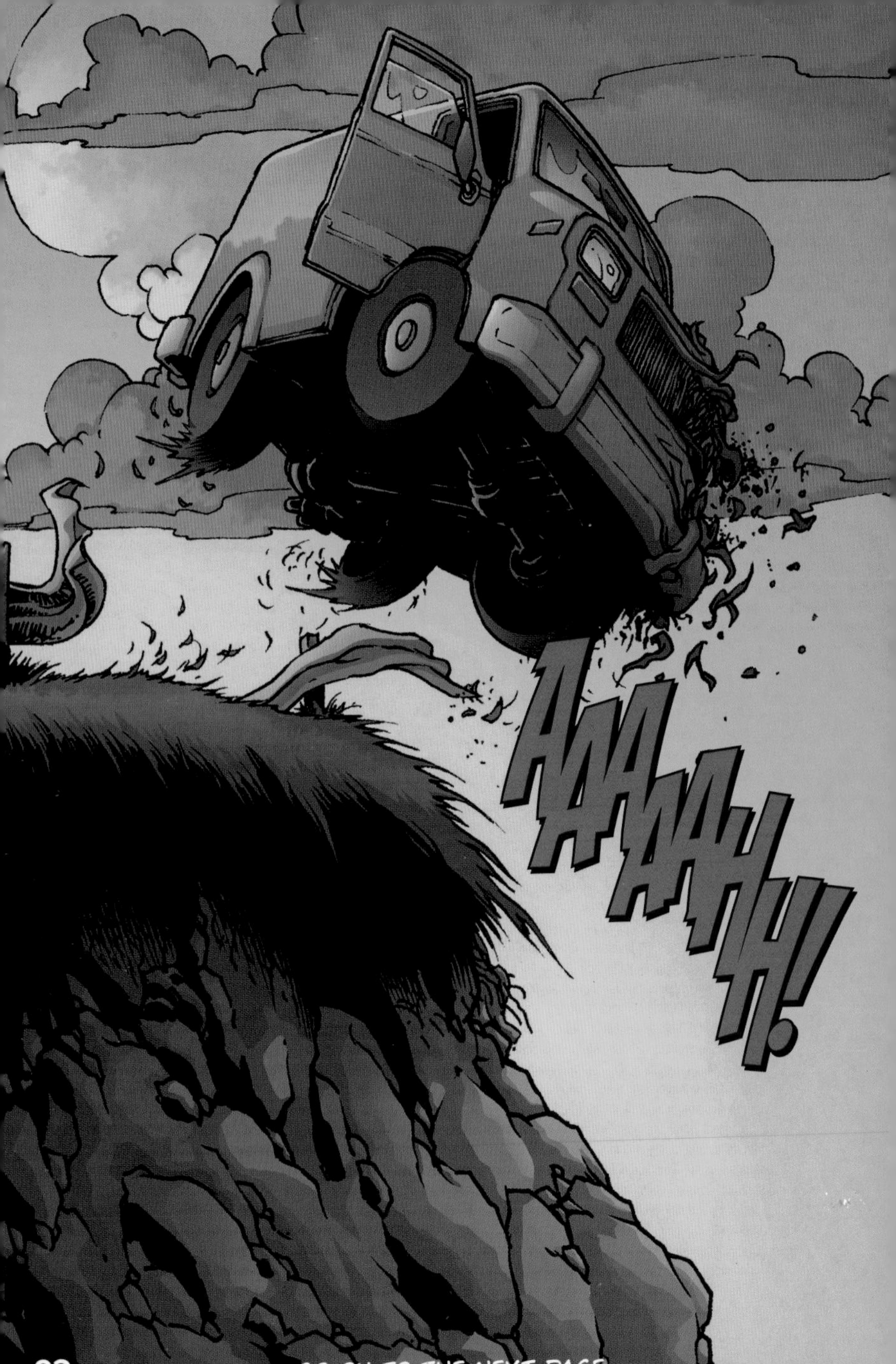
AAAAAAHH!

GO ON TO THE NEXT PAGE.

The van flips end over end as it smashes its way down the hillside. It's a good thing vampires are hard to damage. All the high-tech equipment in the back of the van has come loose and is now flying around in a storm of sharp corners and edges.

For a split second you can see out the front, through the shattered windshield. You're headed straight for a barn. Then there's another impact, larger than the others have been, as you crash straight through the wall of the barn and come to rest below the hayloft.

You can't tell if anybody else is hurt, but you do know one thing: The van is not in direct sunlight. You can get out safely.

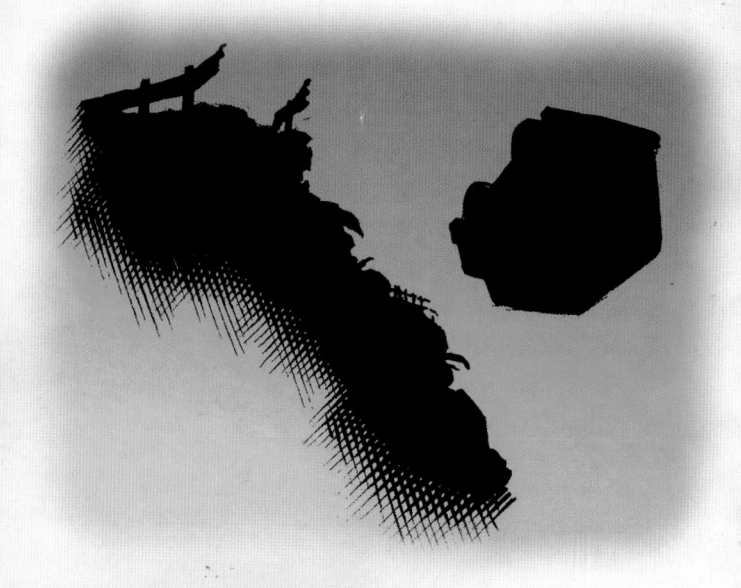

TURN TO PAGE 21.

Danforth steps forward, amazed. "But that's great!" he says excitedly. "That's what we're here to investigate—the unfair treatment of vampires in the media! We could make a documentary!"

You can't believe it. "You—you mean you *want* to show vampires in a positive light?"

He starts to nod . . .

. . . but then a tall, silver-haired man in a suit bursts into the room! Everyone jumps, startled. The stranger is panting and clutching at his side, but he's got a huge grin on his face. "At last!" he says, his eyes wild. "Caught, right out in the open, by *me!* Adam Limburger Focaccia Jr.—vampire hunter!"

He reaches behind him and pulls a gigantic gun out of his waistband. "Try this on for size!" he shouts. "Bullets filled with holy water and *coated* in *garlic oil!* I'll kill you *and* these filthy vampire supporters!"

The group seems caught off guard by this weirdo just as much as you are.

WILL YOU...

...shepherd the humans away from him so you can show them the way out?

TURN TO PAGE 110.

...go after Focaccia and trust the LaTour family to take care of themselves?

TURN TO PAGE 50.

THERE THEY ARE. YOU'LL BE RIGHT ON TOP OF THEM IN SECONDS.

BUT WHY AREN'T THEY RUNNING AND HIDING?

WHAT ARE THEY DOING IN THERE?

SOMETHING'S NOT RIGHT.

BUT YOU'RE WAY TOO ANGRY AT PROFESSOR GUMPERT TO HOLD BACK NOW.

GO ON TO THE NEXT PAGE.

Graciela now stands in the middle of the kitchen. She's just standing there, shivering, looking straight at you. *Obviously petrified with fear,* you think. Not that she needs to be. You're furious with the professor, not her or her husband.

The woman still hasn't moved as you pass through the doorway of the kitchen—and suddenly you're sprayed with some sort of sticky, gooey liquid! Your wings stick to your sides, and you fall with a thud.

"Bull's-eye!" the professor screams. He's holding something like a metal squirt gun. "Dead center with the Ultra-Glue!"

You try to escape—but you're stuck to the floor!

The professor looms over you, a long, sharp stake in one hand, and smiles evilly. "Say good-bye, monster." He sneers.

And then the stake drives down.

THE END

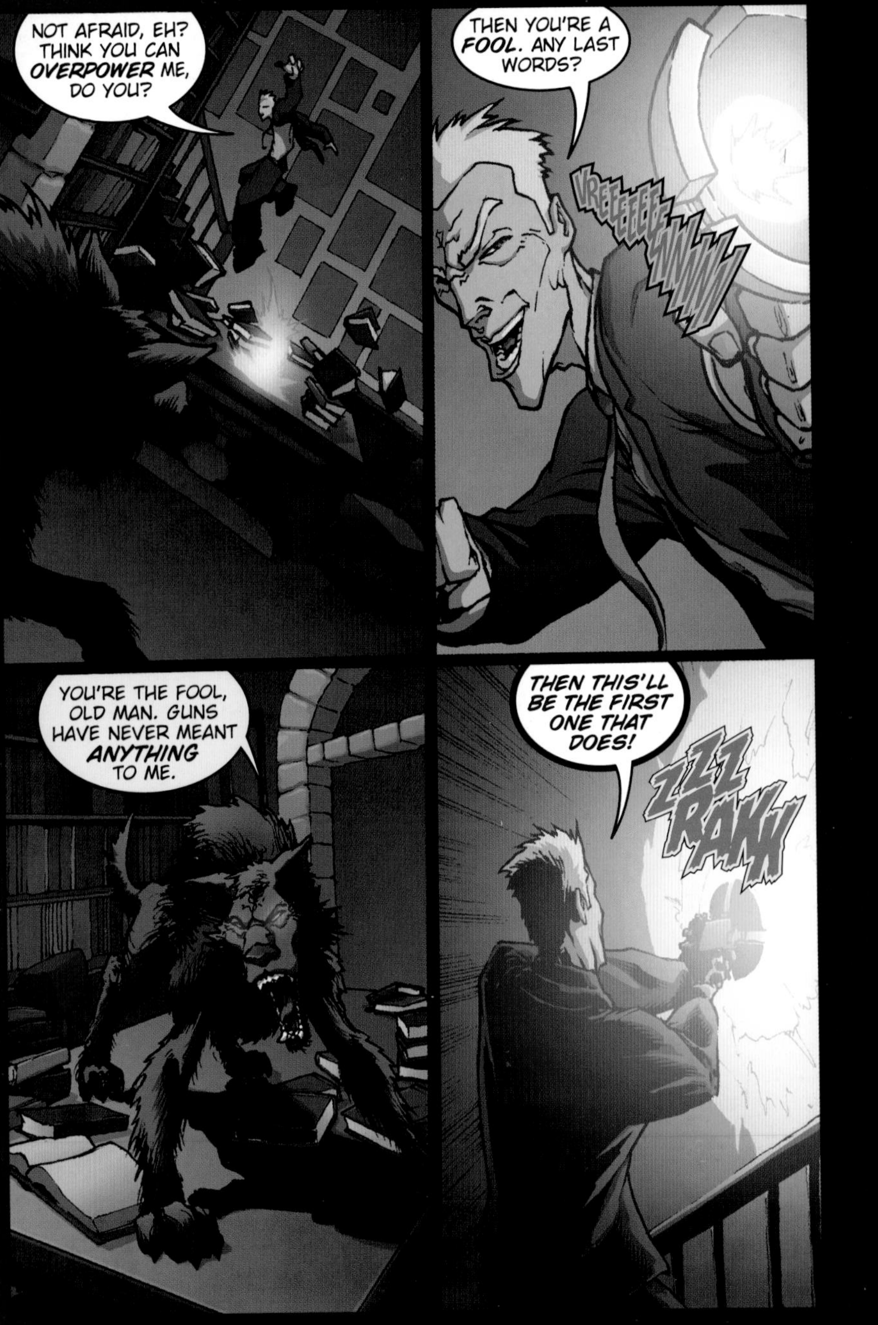
NOT AFRAID, EH? THINK YOU CAN **OVERPOWER** ME, DO YOU?
THEN YOU'RE A **FOOL**. ANY LAST WORDS?
VREEEEEEEENNNNN
YOU'RE THE FOOL, OLD MAN. GUNS HAVE NEVER MEANT **ANYTHING** TO ME.
THEN THIS'LL BE THE FIRST ONE THAT DOES!
ZZZ RAKK

GO ON TO THE NEXT PAGE.

You've never seen a brighter, more glaring, more *painful* flash of light in your life. You close your eyes, but it doesn't make any difference. The light flares straight through your eyelids. And when you can see again, you notice a big ugly scorch mark on the wall right next to where you were standing.

Focaccia's still on the other side of the room, and the sun gun starts to make that whiny power-up sound again. "You should've run away while you had the opportunity!" he says, gloating. "I've widened the beam, so there's no way I can miss now! You're about to be turned into ash!"

You start to say, "Not if I can transform into mist fast enough," but you only get out the words "not if" before the gun goes off again.

And he's right. He doesn't miss.

THE END

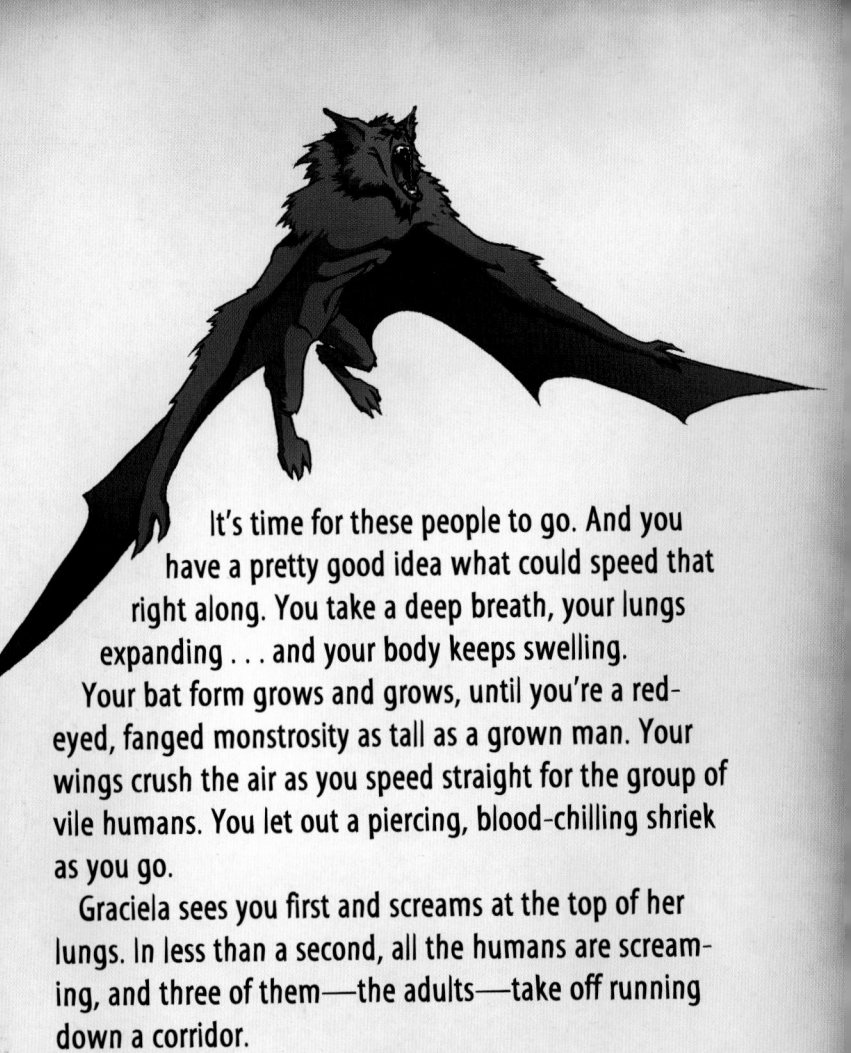

It's time for these people to go. And you
have a pretty good idea what could speed that
right along. You take a deep breath, your lungs
expanding . . . and your body keeps swelling.

Your bat form grows and grows, until you're a red-
eyed, fanged monstrosity as tall as a grown man. Your
wings crush the air as you speed straight for the group of
vile humans. You let out a piercing, blood-chilling shriek
as you go.

Graciela sees you first and screams at the top of her
lungs. In less than a second, all the humans are screaming, and three of them—the adults—take off running
down a corridor.

It's working!

100   GO ON TO THE NEXT PAGE.

You've got these home invaders on the run.

WILL YOU...

. . . go after the ones who
turned and ran?

TURN TO PAGE 89.

. . . land and concentrate on
the ones too scared to move?

TURN TO PAGE 38.

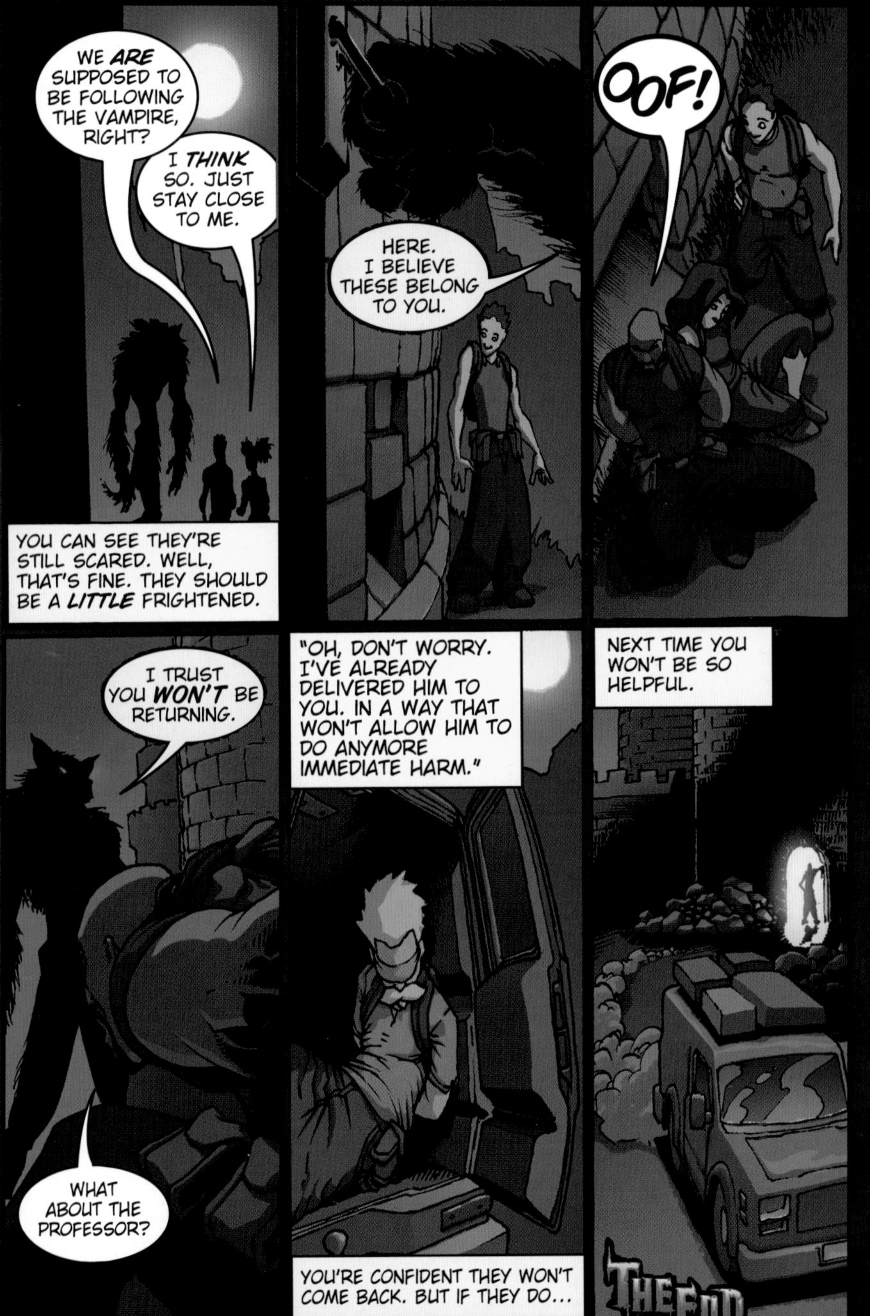
WE ARE SUPPOSED TO BE FOLLOWING THE VAMPIRE, RIGHT?
I THINK SO. JUST STAY CLOSE TO ME.
YOU CAN SEE THEY'RE STILL SCARED. WELL, THAT'S FINE. THEY SHOULD BE A LITTLE FRIGHTENED.
HERE. I BELIEVE THESE BELONG TO YOU.
OOF!
I TRUST YOU WON'T BE RETURNING.
WHAT ABOUT THE PROFESSOR?
"OH, DON'T WORRY. I'VE ALREADY DELIVERED HIM TO YOU. IN A WAY THAT WON'T ALLOW HIM TO DO ANYMORE IMMEDIATE HARM."
YOU'RE CONFIDENT THEY WON'T COME BACK. BUT IF THEY DO...
NEXT TIME YOU WON'T BE SO HELPFUL.
THE END

This guy just won't stop!

You sprint down to the end of a certain corridor, where the hallway ends in a big, heavy door. And as Focaccia comes rushing up . . .

"You're mine now, vampire!" he snarls. "Don't move!"

Like a matador in a bullfight, you step aside at the last minute. Focaccia rockets past you, right through the door you've just pulled open. He screams as he falls ten feet and thumps onto the grass . . .

. . . *outside the castle.*

"You think you can just *throw me out?*" he shouts. "This is outrageous!"

"Outrageous or not, I'm locking all the doors and windows with the power of my mind. There's no way you, or anyone else, can get in now."

Past Focaccia's shouts, you hear the sound of the LaTours' van as they drive away. You're glad they're safe . . . but what a lousy night!

Maybe you'll just go back to bed.

THE END

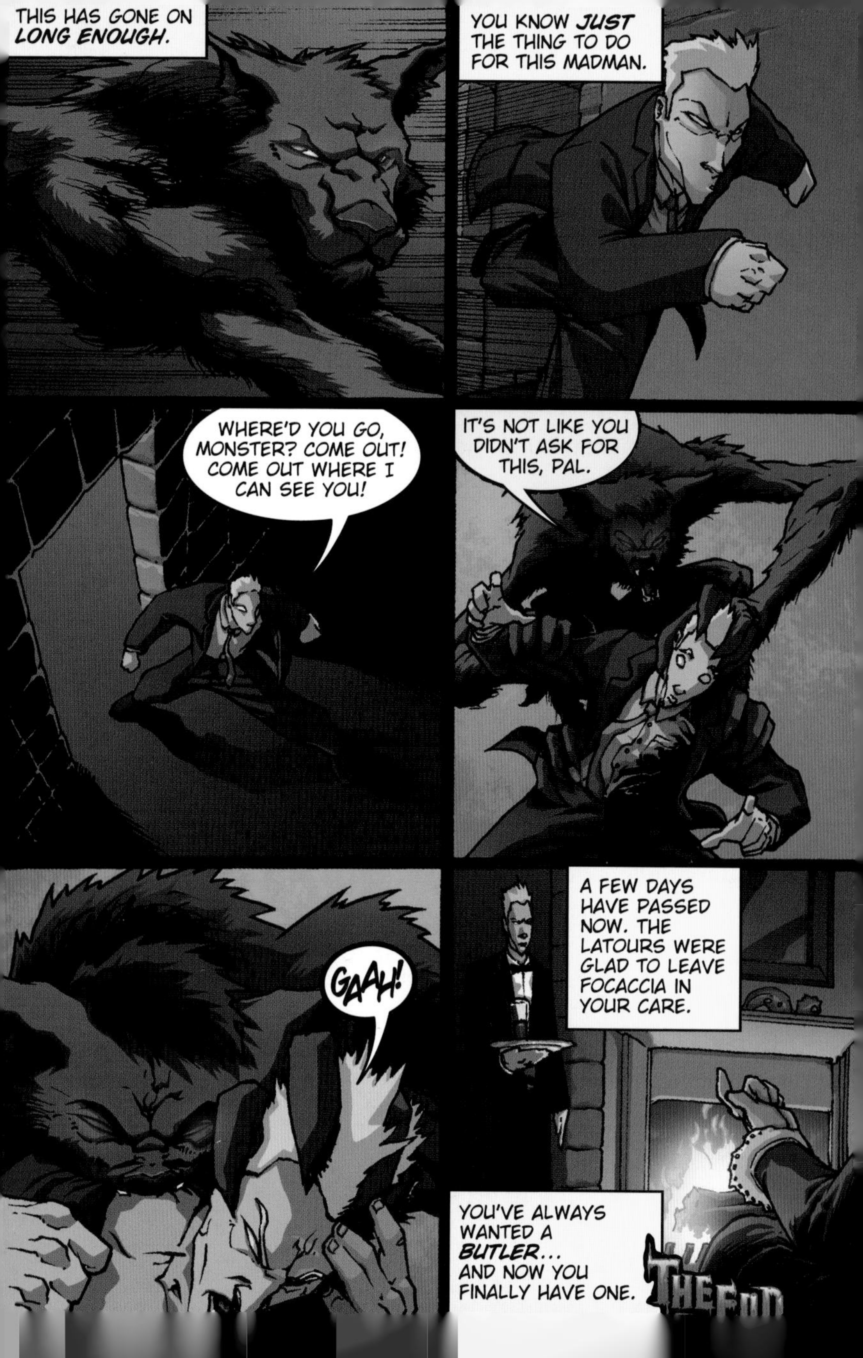
THIS HAS GONE ON **LONG ENOUGH**.
YOU KNOW ***JUST*** THE THING TO DO FOR THIS MADMAN.
WHERE'D YOU GO, MONSTER? COME OUT! COME OUT WHERE I CAN SEE YOU!
IT'S NOT LIKE YOU DIDN'T ASK FOR THIS, PAL.
GAAH!
A FEW DAYS HAVE PASSED NOW. THE LATOURS WERE GLAD TO LEAVE FOCACCIA IN YOUR CARE.
YOU'VE ALWAYS WANTED A ***BUTLER***... AND NOW YOU FINALLY HAVE ONE.
THE END

"I appreciate the offer," you tell them graciously. "I've often thought about going abroad . . . seeing the world."

"It would be so awesome if you came with us!" Jason says. He's your biggest fan, now that he knows you saved him from being turned into a vampire against his will.

But you shake your head. "I've lived my whole life in and around this castle. This is my home. I wouldn't know what to do anywhere else. I'm sorry, but I'm going to have to decline your very generous offer."

The humans are sad, but they understand. They promise to go back and make an official report that the castle  was destroyed. "That ought to keep people from bothering you," they say.

You're a little sad to see them go . . . but it sure will be nice to get back to some peace and quiet.

THE END

You hit the ground fifty feet
behind the two teenagers
and their father, ready to dish out some massive damage. They don't even know you're there yet. Your breath
rumbles in a barely contained roar, and your claws dig up
chunks of earth as you pick up speed.

But even as you're about to pounce and rip into them,
you hear the boy talking . . .

"Do you think we'll get anything on video, Dad?" he
asks.

"I don't know, son," Danforth answers. "We can only do
our best and hope it's good enough."

Jason speaks again: "Do you think the professor will be
mad when he finds out why we're really here?"

The boy's father shrugs. "I don't know that either. He
might be. But it doesn't matter."

What's this? More secrets? Intrigued, you drop back,
observing even more keenly.

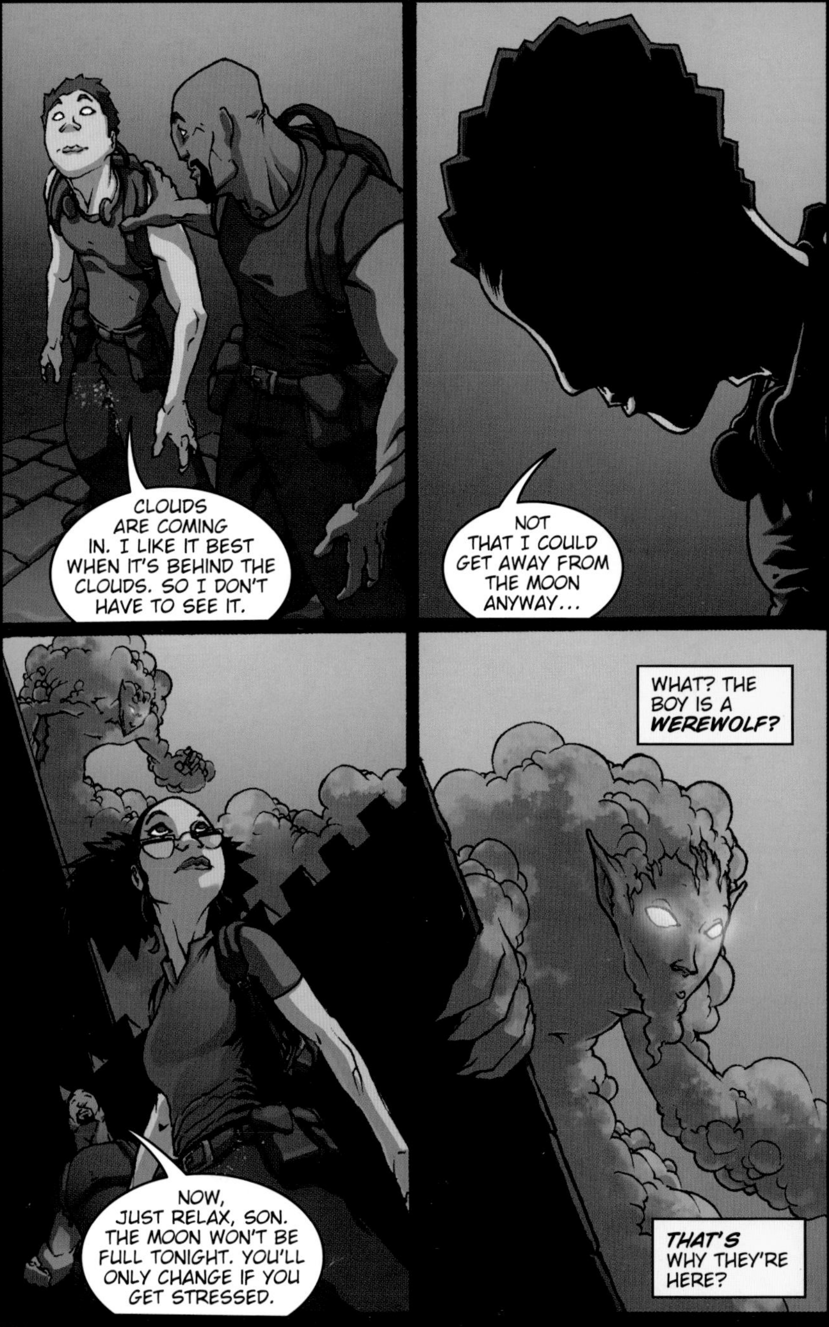

CLOUDS ARE COMING IN. I LIKE IT BEST WHEN IT'S BEHIND THE CLOUDS. SO I DON'T HAVE TO SEE IT.
NOT THAT I COULD GET AWAY FROM THE MOON ANYWAY...
NOW, JUST RELAX, SON. THE MOON WON'T BE FULL TONIGHT. YOU'LL ONLY CHANGE IF YOU GET STRESSED.
WHAT? THE BOY IS A ***WEREWOLF?***
THAT'S WHY THEY'RE HERE?

GO ON TO THE NEXT PAGE.

So the humans have brought a *werewolf* to your castle. But why? Do they mean to hurt you? Or could they have some other reason?

WILL YOU...

...offer to help them?
TURN TO PAGE 12.

...go on the offensive and attack the werewolf?
TURN TO PAGE 61.

...decide you've have enough of this whole business and do something *really* drastic?
TURN TO PAGE 47.

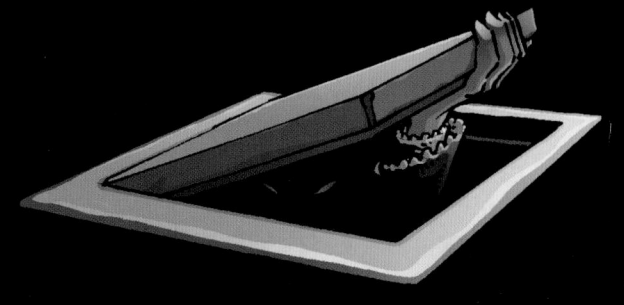

It's funny: You tell Morton Zoffo, the head producer, that you can only go out at night, but that doesn't bother him at all. "That's when everything happens anyway, baby!" he says.

And boy, does Morton deliver on his promises! He hooks you up with a top-notch talent agent, and all of a sudden, you're doing guest appearances on talk shows, you've got commercial endorsement deals . . . then you get offered the starring role in a movie! The director loves you, because you can do all your own stunts. As long as there's no garlic around, you pretty much can't be hurt.

Soon other vampires start coming out into the public eye too. "You're a pioneer!" they tell you. "You made people understand that we're not bad guys after all!"

And as you relax in your Bel-Air mansion, you can't help but think, *I could've done a lot worse with my life.*

THE END

"Come on," you whisper urgently to the professor. "Follow me! I'll get you out of here!" You dart past him, whipping down a side corridor, and hear the rest of the group running after you.

"I say!" the professor huffs, barely keeping up. "This is quite odd, don't you think? A vampire helping a bunch of humans?"

"Does that Focaccia fellow strike you as mentally unstable?" you reply. "Dangerous, even?"

"Well . . . yes."

"Me too. But you and your people don't. So come on."

The six of you make a quick turn. You press a hidden panel and open a doorway to a secret passage.

You hear Focaccia closing in. "There's no use running! I'll have all your heads for trophies!"

He's too late, though. You hurry everyone inside and shut the door before he can get there.

GO ON TO THE NEXT PAGE.

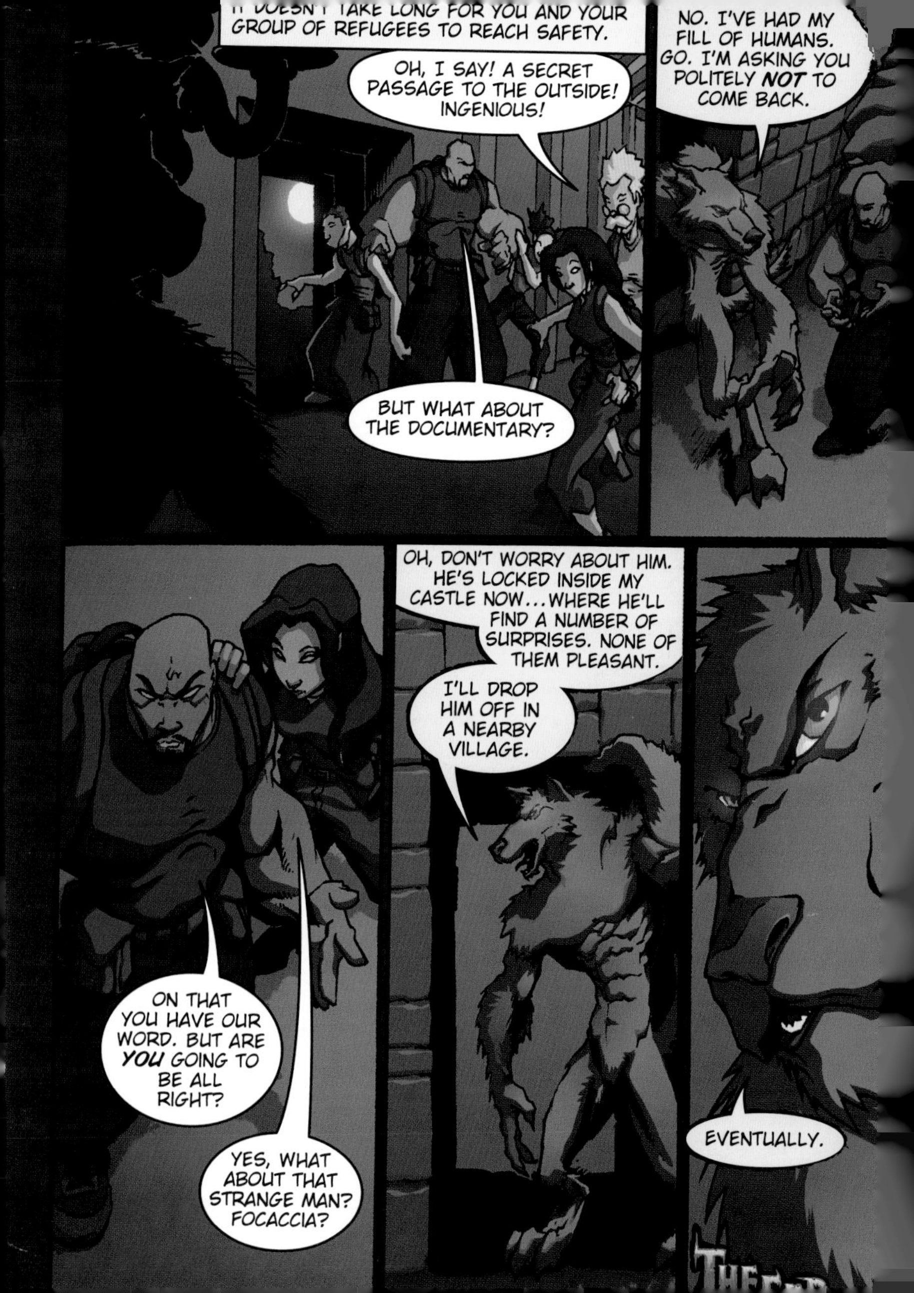

IT DOESN'T TAKE LONG FOR YOU AND YOUR GROUP OF REFUGEES TO REACH SAFETY.
OH, I SAY! A SECRET PASSAGE TO THE OUTSIDE! INGENIOUS!
BUT WHAT ABOUT THE DOCUMENTARY?
NO. I'VE HAD MY FILL OF HUMANS. GO. I'M ASKING YOU POLITELY **NOT** TO COME BACK.
ON THAT YOU HAVE OUR WORD. BUT ARE ***YOU*** GOING TO BE ALL RIGHT?
YES, WHAT ABOUT THAT STRANGE MAN? FOCACCIA?
OH, DON'T WORRY ABOUT HIM. HE'S LOCKED INSIDE MY CASTLE NOW...WHERE HE'LL FIND A NUMBER OF SURPRISES. NONE OF THEM PLEASANT.
I'LL DROP HIM OFF IN A NEARBY VILLAGE.
EVENTUALLY.

WHICH TWISTED JOURNEYS WILL YOU TRY NEXT?

#1 CAPTURED BY PIRATES
A band of scurvy pirates has boarded your ship. Can you keep them from turning you into shark bait?

#2 ESCAPE FROM PYRAMID X
You're on a visit to a pyramid, complete with ancient mummies. But not everything that's ancient is dead . . .

#3 TERROR IN GHOST MANSION
You're trapped in a creepy old house on Halloween with a bunch of spooks. And they aren't wearing costumes . . .

#4 THE TREASURE OF MOUNT FATE
Can you survive the monsters and magic of Mount Fate and bring home its treasure?

#5 NIGHTMARE ON ZOMBIE ISLAND
Legend says no one escapes Zombie Island. Will you be the first? Or will this nightmare be your last?

#6 THE TIME TRAVEL TRAP
Dinosaurs, Wild West train robbers, robots . . . Danger is everywhere when you're caught in a time machine!

#7 VAMPIRE HUNT
Vampire hunters are creeping through an ancient castle. And you're the vampire they're hunting!

#8 ALIEN INCIDENT ON PLANET J
Make peace with the Makaknuk, Zirifubi, and Frongo, or you'll never get off their planet . . .